Jeremy Chikalto
and the
Hazy Souls

T.S. DeBrosse

Published by Viral Cat Press
San Francisco, CA

ISBN: 0615464815
ISBN-13: 9780615464817

Printed in the United States of America.

"Each man is haunted until his humanity awakens."

– WILLIAM BLAKE

ACKNOWLEDGMENTS

I would like to give thanks to my family and friends. Thanks especially to my sister, Danielle, my cousin, Patricia, and to my friends, Taryn and Joanna, for igniting my imagination through childhood play. Thanks also to actor Jeff Goldblum for his very real, albeit bizarre and unconventional, influence on Jeremy. Thanks to my readers at San Francisco State, especially Robert Gluck, Dodie Bellamy, and Elizabeth Black. And a special thanks to my husband, Jesse, who believed in my story and helped sharpen my prose, and to my children, Mirabelle, Faline, and Lachlan.

PART 1

CHAPTER 1

CHOIR SONG

Lyrna coughed up a fur ball. "Don't run from the brush next time," said Jeremy, as he placed the dappled gray fizdruft on the marble floor. A fizdruft was like a talking house cat, except it could decapitate you in a second if mishandled. But Jeremy Chikalto knew how to handle a fizdruft. You have to pick it up by one ear, grabbing only the endmost tuft of fur. Thanks to a peculiar bundle of nerves stimulated in this way, the wild fizdruft would then become tame. Only then would it be safe to support its bottom.

Lyrna licked her fur down and watched Jeremy uneasily, always vigilant. "Much ready?"

"Plenty ready. I'm just sort of fixating, Lyrna. But I like to see my fixations through."

It was rumored in Watico that once a fizdruft was tamed, it would protect its owner by detecting evil presences (Lyrna called them "bad bads"). This was why Jeremy Chikalto needed a fizdruft. Jeremy was the Royal Cajjez of Watico and so was entitled to any object or creature he desired. He asked

1

for Lyrna eight years ago following a series of unexplained phenomena.

Jeremy tore through the top drawer of his dresser for the third time, his mind cycling through a list of affirmations: *They love me. I'm not crazy. Everyone's there for me. Not. Crazy.*

The door to his bedroom burst open, and his father, Wantoro, entered, inching through the frame sideways because his shoulders were too wide with all the royal tassels. "Jeremy! Get out there. Now. You've got five minutes!"

Jeremy narrowed his sapphire eyes, an untamed energy flashing behind moonbeam irises, then: occlusion. "Can't find them." He shrugged.

"Can't find what?"

"Purple gloves." It didn't matter to Jeremy that it didn't matter to his father. Sometimes simple objects contained meaning, which when finally realized, lent an air of poetry to life.

His father sputtered. "Purple gloves? You're late to the Watican Awards Opening Ceremony because you want your hands decorated?"

Lyrna circled Jeremy's feet, then dropped the purple gloves.

"She's found them! Fortuitous, dear father. What's that Earth saying? Virgil, Latin: 'Audentis fortuna iuvat.' Fortune favors the bold." Jeremy scooped up the gloves and then slapped them against his thigh.

"Well hurry up then. You've got the concert, the reenactment, the dance, then the awards—if you could just," Wantoro squeezed his hands into balls, "pull off one day, with no nonsense, please, it's all I'm asking. You're fifteen now, you're perfectly capable." He released his fists from their tight coils. "I'm taking my seat. Be down soon." Wantoro stomped out the door.

Jeremy patted Lyrna on the head and then held up his purple gloves, which were embroidered with the Chikalto crest. The gloves were silky, elegant, and cool to the touch. He slipped his hands through and rubbed them together, relishing the buttery slip and slap. "These ridiculous things are everything."

"Fancy," said Lyrna, hopping from paw to paw.

"Very. Think Maren will be impressed?" Jeremy mock flexed his gloved hands and grunted in a display of strength. He laughed.

Lyrna's tongue dumbly licked her eye.

"You know purple holds special significance to me." Jeremy stared thoughtfully at his gloves. "Hey Lyrna?"

She meowed.

"It's been three days." Jeremy quieted, his mood shifting once more. *It's going to happen again soon. God, it's suffocating.* "I'll get this over with. It'll be fun. Best day, and all."

"Yes." Lyrna leapt up into his arms and he squeezed her and closed his eyes.

Jeremy set Lyrna down and then drew back the velvet curtains to his balcony, unlocked the window, and looked out. Below, the crowd in the concert hall anticipated his entrance. Jeremy smiled. His concerts elevated him, helped him to forget his inadequacies, and quieted his dread of the unknown, which had been building in recent weeks.

Three-thousand guests filled the Watican Hall. A few people were still arriving through the high-arched doorways, the sparkling gold and silver interior glinting off their jewelry and watches. A stage overlooked the hall, a platform carved from the slab of an enormous tree, gleaming with the dull shine of years.

"Cajjez Jeremy Chikalto!" announced the Senior Conductor of the Watican Heldelsa Choir, who was standing at the center of the stage. The conductor was a waify, nervous man, whose mustache twitched at the very mention of the Cajjez.

The conductor's wife sat in the VIP box to the far left of the stage, her nails digging into the back of the chair next to her. Maren Nononia, Jeremy's Guest of Honor, cried out.

"Ow! You've got my hair!"

"Sorry, love." The conductor's wife released Maren's wavy, dark blonde tresses.

Maren shaded her brow with her hand and scanned the stage for Jeremy. He was late. Guests were beginning to shift in their seats. Maren glanced beside her and saw that Jeremy's mother, Vinya Raacyhila Chikalto, was appraising her. "I'm sure he'll be out soon," she said, her cheeks flushing. Jeremy's mother, like Jeremy, was a gifted singer and dancer. Maren was terrified she'd disappoint the Vinya later in the evening when she was set to dance with Jeremy. No doubt that's why Raaychila was appraising her. Maren was a trained dancer, but she was no prodigy like Jeremy. Would she slip and ruin the performance? Would she crowd the stage? Jeremy had an unwavering commitment to take up as much space as possible, charismatic but dangerous. He was intoxicating, and she knew as their ages continued to climb, the allure would only intensify.

Raaychila rose from her seat, her sharp features drawn together in worry. "Will you excuse me for a second?" she asked, squeezing past Maren, brushing her with her emerald silk gown.

Raaychila's husband, Vor Wantoro Chikalto, motioned to his excitable wife to sit down. "Raaychila, I just talked to him. Sit. Get comfortable."

"CAJJEZ JEREMY CHIKALTO!" yelled the conductor.

Jeremy appeared at the stage door and was met with thunderous applause. He crossed the stage, allowing the spotlight overhead to follow him at a leisurely pace. He waved his purple-gloved hand and bowed.

The conductor lifted his baton and a hush swept over the audience. Jeremy stepped up to the mic, his broad smile amplifying his star-shine. "Welcome, Ladies and Gentlemen, to the Annual Watican Awards Opening Ceremony, honoring outstanding achievement in Earth Studies. We thank the Nononias for their continued support in spreading peace and goodwill throughout the Farmoore Galaxy, and for their generous foundation, which makes this event possible."

The audience applauded. Maren Nononia turned and waved to her parents, who sat in the row behind her.

"And now," continued Jeremy, "'Vordin's Dream,' a Watican hymn dating back to the first years of Farmoore's creation." The conductor set his baton in motion and Jeremy's treble voice ascended like a dove and sang:

> Like storm clouds' onslaught,
> You've beaten back the Light.
> Lesser souls would have you reconciled,
> And urge you to abandon those rebel storms,
> And transmit the light like the blue day.
> They know not; a jilted lover in you rages
> And the wedding guests sway in sad neglect–
> The celestial space invites the angel-child
> to wonder as an outcast prays,
> to repeat a history
> and bow to an impious might.

Let the cinders fall where they may,
A Kingdom awaits, the balm of vague unrest.

Jeremy stopped singing. The great, stringed vindevo struck a minor chord, championing in the chorus line, but it was absent of its singer. The conductor frantically motioned to his players, *hold the measure!,* but it was no use. Under the spotlight, Jeremy cocked his head to the side, eyes vacant, lips parted, floating away.

The air rippled, cracked with static, and then tore open inches from Jeremy's face. A buzzing pushed against his brain and he leaned into it, finally whispering, "Do you see?" *This was it,* he thought. This was the moment he'd waited for–his proof, his validation, and that most pressing question, what was behind? "Can you see the air?" he said into the mic. The music quieted. "It's in front of me and I don't know how to control it," he said, louder, groping the void. "This is what I've been saying!"

The audience began to murmur. Words like 'mad,' 'delusional,' and 'bizarre' rose and fell, a wave crashing on the prospects of Jeremy's future. Then the air stopped twitching, the buzzing lifted, and Jeremy saw the audience clearly, some lost in confusion and others giddy with a petty sort of power, a well of gossip ready to spill over at first opportunity. A pit formed in Jeremy's chest, black and roiling, as he realized: no one saw. Jeremy cursed, turned, and ran off the stage.

Chapter 2

Air

There was a knock on the door.

Jeremy sat on the floor, leaning back on the silk comforter draped over his bed, with Lyrna on his lap. "Come in." It would be his mom, he knew, and she'd have put tablets into his drink.

Raaychila entered, cradling two bowls of toffee and a strong feltzor tea. "I hope you're okay? I've brought toffee." Raaychila let out a nervous laugh. Her sea-green eyes were shiny from recent tears.

"Toffee! I toffee!" mewed Lyrna, and she began to purr.

"Thanks for the toffee, Mom. I'll just need a minute."

Raaychila set the two bowls down in front of Lyrna and Jeremy, and then folded her arms across her chest. "You brought up the air again. We can work through this. It's going to be okay. Are you feeling sick? Do you need to see the doctor? And that first verse–oh, it was beautiful. I'm so proud." She ran her hands through her hair. "But don't worry about the concert, all anyone can talk about is that note where you slid up two octaves, and, well–"

"Do you even want the truth?" Jeremy shot her a nasty look. "Do you hear yourself? 'All anyone noticed…?' I know what they noticed."

Lyrna growled as she ate, the tufts of black fur on the tips of her ears bobbing up and down.

"Such a loud chewer, Lyrna," said Jeremy irritably.

"Jeremy. I'm so proud and I mean that. We have a tight schedule today. If you have to make some adjustments, no worries, we've planned for this. Just let me know." She allowed a moment of silence to tempt Jeremy into conversation. He didn't take the bait. "So you don't want to talk about what happened on the stage?"

"No."

"Did you experience, like, a head pressure, and the tingling sensation? Because honestly it looked like a migraine, and that can be explained. Remember how Dr. Levison said stress can be a trigger?"

"Yeah, can you leave?" Jeremy drummed his fingers on his drugged tea.

Raaychila sighed. "I will respect your wishes. We'll talk later, and take as much time as you need." She gently closed the door behind her.

"Air again?" mewed Lyrna. She tugged at the pillow in Jeremy's arms, hoping to replace it with her own warm, furry body.

"I had a feeling it would happen today. And it was intense, Lyrna, it tore open!" He set his pillow down and began pacing his room. "I just… I thought everyone had seen this time. But I *am* crazy, aren't I?" He bit his lip and braced himself for the verdict.

Lyrna tucked her ears back. "Not."

"You've seen the air twitch, right? 100%, not just loyal-pet-yessing me?"

"Yessing because yes."

Jeremy stared at the air in front of him. If only he could will it to happen, right now, while he was prepared. "Come on air, whatever you are." He breathed in deeply and focused on a spot ten inches from his face. Everything blurred together, the war tapestries on his walls, the book shelves with tall ladders, and the large window open to a morning sky. Jeremy focused on a point. For a second, he thought he felt a zap. Then, nothing. He shook his head, yelled obscenities, grabbed his pillow, and hurled it at the wall. A picture that his mother painted crashed to the floor, scattering shards of glass across the marble. The eruption felt good, and his own power flooded him. There was a thrill in being violent, in causing violence, but he swallowed it down.

"Calm," mewed Lyrna.

"I didn't mean to do that, you know I didn't." Jeremy wrapped his arms over his head and suppressed a yell, and the effort made him feel as ill as if he'd swallowed back stomach bile. "I need a breath of fresh air."

CHAPTER 3

THE DIARY

After the Watican Awards Opening Ceremony concluded, Maren excused herself from her parents and walked to Jeremy's wing of the castle. She moved slowly down the carpeted hallway towards Jeremy's room, watching her reflection in the mirrors on the walls. No doubt she'd changed since he last saw her. She was taller now and had lost some of the baby fat in her cheeks. She fancied herself poised, and smiled, but then something shattered somewhere in the castle and she jumped. When she regained her balance, she noticed the family portraits.

Vordin Chikalto. She admired the face in the oil painting, the long, dark blonde hair, the electric blue eyes–*just like Jeremy's.* Jeremy eerily resembled his ancestor, Vordin Chikalto, founder of the Farmoore Galaxy. She blushed at the thought that someday Jeremy might share the physique of Vordin Chikalto, with the swell of muscles under his tunic and broad shoulders. But Jeremy was still boyish and smaller than herself, though they were the same age. She doubted

12

he'd ever be as exalted as his ancestor before him. Jeremy was far too whimsical, far too... unstable. She arrived at his door and knocked.

No answer.

Maren nudged the heavy door open and peered inside the expansive room with vaulted ceilings and chandeliers. She could make out the turret spire in the corner enclave with its impressive view of the east city. Was he looking out the window? But no, Jeremy wasn't there. Lyrna trotted over to her.

"Maren!" Lyrna wove herself around Maren's legs and tugged at the skirt of her dress.

Maren scooped her up using proper technique. "Where's Jeremy?"

Lyrna looked away and wriggled in Maren's arms. "Out walk."

"Okay," said Maren, putting Lyrna down. She knew Lyrna was protective of the Cajjez, and that the fizdruft probably wouldn't elaborate.

Lyrna gave Maren a mew and scurried past the silk comforter to hide under Jeremy's bed.

Maren walked to the window and looked out. *I shouldn't linger*, then she noticed the broken picture frame on the marble floor. His outburst was undoubtedly about the strange end to his performance. It was wrong to lurk in these private spaces; it was wrong to have come. She retreated back towards the door, and a passing thought comforted her. *At least the canvas survived the fall*, a mottled landscape of greens and grays, juxtaposed with bright yellow figures in the foreground. *He probably went to find a maid.* "Lyrna, I'm leaving now. Please tell him I want to talk about our dance later and that I hope it's still on."

But then as she neared the door, Maren's eyes rested on another piece of artwork. The tapestry on the wall behind his bed depicted the ancient battle on Earth that resulted in the creation of the Farmoore Galaxy. God's faithful remained on Earth and the rebels were banished. There was a flash, so the story goes, and everyone woke up far, far away. Vordin Chikalto led the charge against God's people on Earth, though he later repented. *Such a violent tapestry, how can Jeremy sleep with this next to his bed?*

Maren had never been to Earth, though the journey was possible with modern technology. She'd long decided to pursue an academic career in Earth Studies and knew that it was a twenty-five year round-trip journey, and one that was rarely made except by certain ambitious Earth Studies scholars and their families. The Earth observation missions were kept secret because the people from Earth were unaware of the existence of life on other planets. More importantly, they had a habit of destroying or exploiting each other, a practice the Chikalto dynasty strove to reform as part of their penance, and one they were loath to rekindle.

Maren started to tremble. It was against her nature to rebel or act out, but it was entirely in her nature to seek out truth, and here it was: on the bookshelf beside his bed, the spine of a journal read, *Cajjez Jeremy: Events Log.* Maren looked anxiously at the door. Fascinated as she was with Earth Studies, her own private truth was that she didn't believe in the history of the founding of the Farmoore Galaxy. She didn't believe that the ruling class's power was based on some divine lineage. Alluring or not, Jeremy Chikalto was not fit to rule. *Maybe just real quick,* she thought to herself, pulling the book off the shelf. Then, in Latin, the most treasured of Earth Studies languages, she thought: *Audentis fortuna iuvat.* "Fortune favors the bold."

Maren opened the book to a random page. Scribbled in tidy cursive were the thoughts of Jeremy Chikalto:

Incident 57: I was coming out of the dining room, and I saw the air tremble. I accidentally touched a warped spot and went behind the air! There was a bright, purple light, spinning on a center point in space, a vacuum that pulled up or else a vortex that pulled down, and beyond that were rays, some bright as the sun on Ganglesh and others darker than the oil of Maltdun's Crator. I fell back. When I opened my eyes, I had returned to the hallway. The air continued to twitch.

Maren squinted and reread the text. Jeremy had always made strange claims, like the time when he insisted energy had a color. "It's purple!" he yelled. *This is sad. These are delusions.* She'd heard plenty of rumors about the Cajjez's mental fitness, and after today, perhaps the lower courts would apply pressure to institutionalize the Democratic Prehaanon. Jeremy opened the door. Maren slammed the journal shut and looked at him standing in the door frame.

"What are you doing?" asked Jeremy. He crossed the room and yanked the journal from her hand. His calm unsettled her.

"I was... just looking through some of your books, to borrow one. I'm so sorry, I–"

"Interesting choice. Events Log?" he said, reading the title over slowly. "Wonder what thrilling tale of romance is inked on these pages!" He set the book on a table, and then propped his door open with a crystal door-stop before turning to Maren with a faint smile.

Maren let out a nervous laugh, her cheeks turning crimson. "I came looking for you, and well, I let Lyrna know to er, pass on a message to you about..." *What was it I said?* "the dance! But, you're here now, so. Well, I haven't seen you in a while. You look taller," she added hopefully. *I am no rebel. I am not bold.*

"I'm feeling uncomfortable. Are you feeling awkward?" asked Jeremy.

"What? No."

"Because you are." Jeremy grinned, then stepped in front of the door to block her. "What about our dance?"

"First, it's nice to see you, I think. You haven't actually changed much," Maren deadpanned. "And I'm very sorry I looked at your bookshelf. I shouldn't have gone in once I realized you weren't there. I'd like to ask for your forgiveness."

"You'd like to ask for my forgiveness?" Jeremy circled her. "Every year with this formality you throw at me."

"It's respect," she answered, her eyes downcast.

"You think I want respect?" Jeremy dipped low until his eyes caught hers. "I just want to be seen."

Maren took a deep breath. "Yes, of course, I see you. Everyone sees you."

"Right," said Jeremy with a twang of sadness in his voice, and then he vaulted into a back handspring, landed in a crouched position, then slapped his hands on the marble.

Maren jumped. It was just what he did. He bounced off walls. He interjected songs into serious conversations. He laughed. He raged. "If you're feeling up to it, did you want to hang out before the reenactment? First, I mean, I wanted to check in and see if you were okay. You got sick on stage, something. Your mom said a migraine, halo effect with lights? But you seem..., so how are you? I'm so sorry that happens to you. Sounds painful."

Jeremy studied her. "With the sorry again... I'm okay," his voice was kind and soft now, deliberately soft like he was goading her. "Gee, you're sweet checkin' in like that, on the big headache."

This boy is insane. "Could we run through the dance? I've always hated the separate choreography, like it's supposed to all come together seamlessly somehow—"

"Which it does—"

"—and I'd feel more comfortable—"

"—because I lead." Jeremy stuffed his hands in his pockets and smirked.

Maren balled her hands into fists. "I'm just saying I'd feel more comfortable—"

"I'd love to practice our dance, Maren. But you're kidding yourself if you think it'll make you feel more comfortable."

"What's that supposed to mean?" Maren stepped to him. It was more aggressive than she'd ever been in the past, but she was developing a sense of inner confidence and he had no right to pretend to know her.

Jeremy rubbed his neck and then stepped to Maren, mere inches between them. "You want to dance with me in my bedroom? Should I dim the lights?"

A great warmth flushed through Maren, turning her molten hot, and she rushed toward the door. "We don't have to practice the dance. We'll just wing it, I guess." She walked out of his room before he could respond.

Chapter 4

The Re-enactment

Jeremy grabbed his journal and lay on his bed, rereading old entries and trying to imagine what Maren thought. He hoped she hadn't read much. "This is bad, Lyrna. She read something crazy. It's all crazy."

After a while, a maid came in with a tray of tea sandwiches and fintin juice. She studied him cautiously. "Feeling alright, Cajjez?"

"Yes, fine." He swatted her away. "Thanks, Stella. Am I being checked in on? Checked. In. On." Jeremy used his finger to mark the punctuation between the words. "That's weird to say."

"Are your cheeks hot? They look red."

Jeremy felt his cheeks. "Kind of invasive," he muttered. "I'm fine, I'm just embarrassed. It's nothing."

The maid bowed. "Of course, Cajjez."

Jeremy returned to the journal, and soon found himself rifling through Events Log 2 and 3. When exactly had that static sensation started? It felt especially strong this morning. He looked at the clock on the wall. *I'm late!* "Lyrna! I almost missed the reenactment," he called out. "Crazy at the concert, rude to Maren, and now let's add tardy to my checklist for this most important day. My dad wasn't wrong. No poetry in his life, sure, but he wasn't wrong about me."

Lyrna only said, "Be nice, self!"

Jeremy changed into his undergarments, a white silk top and brown cotton pants. His armor would be backstage at the arena. Why hadn't the maid reminded him to get ready? He'd have plenty of time later to dwell on the air and his embarrassment on stage, plus Maren's wayward reading adventure. The reenactment would work as a reset, and Jeremy needed it.

Jeremy dashed out of his room in his undergarments and slippers, wound his way through the castle corridors (guards merely waving in surprise), and exited to a path outside leading to the arena. As he ran along the cobblestones to that grand, bowl-shaped stadium, he could hear the crowd's excitement. *What's going on?* Jeremy reached the stairwell to the backstage area, flung open the door, and bounded up the stairs as the commotion grew louder. He came to the backstage door at the middle level of the arena and could now look out at the playing field.

The arena was staged to look like a desert plain baked by the sun. Two armies were gathering. On one side were bearded men in animal skins holding spears and slings. They were banging wooden shields and shouting "Yahweh!" The other camp gathered in silence except for the clanging of iron armor. On a signal, they drew swords and knocked arrows. The front line of armored men formed a wall of shields and slid lances through the gaps.

The sea of iron parted in the center and Vordin Chikalto, the founder of the Farmoore Galaxy, cantered to the front of the line on a white horse. He was resplendent in white chainmail and wore the helm of a hawk over his long blonde hair. In his hand he swung a massive flail.

Jeremy's jaw dropped. They got his understudy to play Vordin Chikalto?! That was *his* role! Jeremy refused to watch from the sidelines. He burst through the backstage door, pushed past a few guards, and threw on a spare suit of armor sitting in the costume area. He fussed with the clips and straps for a moment, then decided it was good enough.

"Cajjez Chikalto?" said a guard. "Jeremy? We were told—" began another.

Jeremy plopped a blonde wig over his head, fitted a helmet over that, then grabbed a flail from a weapon rack leaning against the wall. He belted on a sword for good measure, then exited the dressing room and jogged through a hallway.

Jeremy stepped onto the arena's desert plain and winced as the setting sun shone brightly in his face. The reenactment was almost at the finale.

"Is this it, then?" shouted the Vordin Chikalto understudy. "The blessing of the Lord is a curse on the righteous, and his curse is a blessing for the fool! In his mercy he is cruel, and in his cruelty he is merciful. Since I defied you by showing mercy, am I in your graces for butchering your people? And what does the Lord love more than an offering of flesh?"

Vordin swung his flail, and the iron men marched forward. Jeremy ran into the battle from the shoulder, also swinging his flail. The men in animal skins began to look back and forth, unsure of the two Vordins, then roared and charged the wall of lances. Arrows and rocks crisscrossed the sky. Then a blimp floating above the arena unleashed bolts of lightning, and there was a sound like the air being torn asunder, and black smoke swirled onto the battlefield. All fighting ceased as the soldiers looked awestruck at the smoke. Except for Jeremy. He continued to spin his flail in intricate patterns, and then pointed it at the imposter Vordin.

The understudy backed up his horse and looked anxiously to Wantoro and Raaychila's raised booth in the audience. A spotlight illuminated Jeremy and the understudy.

Jeremy drew closer, still pointing his flail, and held out his other hand. "Toss me your helmet. I'm Vordin."

But the understudy hesitated.

Jeremy threw his flail to the ground and unsheathed his fencing sword. "Then I'll take it. Dismount and face me. We'll see who is Vordin."

"Uh, is that you, Cajjez? We probably shouldn't…" whispered the understudy, covering his microphone.

"No one can hear me, just go with it."

So the lad climbed off his horse and held out the flail tentatively. Jeremy circled the understudy in expert form, bouncing on the balls of his feet. Then he thrust to the right side of the chest, and the understudy grunted and barely got his flail up in time to deflect the attack. Again, Jeremy cut to the right and smacked the flail. The understudy was panting. Now Jeremy feinted to the right, and the flail came up, but Jeremy spun his sword around to the left, whipping the understudy's wrist with the thin blade.

"Ouch!" cried the Vordin understudy, the microphone booming his voice around the arena, and he dropped his weapon in the dirt.

"Aha," cried Jeremy, leaping forward and hooking his foot around the understudy's heel while driving into his chest with an outstretched palm, and the lad crashed onto the ground.

Jeremy snatched the understudy's helmet triumphantly, and then donned it on his own head while tossing the leftover costume helmet onto his fallen foe. "What's this?!"

he cried, raising his voice. "Have I stirred a rift with God?" he said, pointing to the black smoke that had appeared.

The iron armor and swords of Vordin's army rattled, and hundreds of men drifted towards the black pool of smoke in the center of the arena, where a trap door opened up, leading the actors off stage. Jeremy also drifted ostentatiously into the black smoke. In a woosh, the staged army was sucked into the rift, and it closed. The people of Yahweh fell to the ground and worshipped the One. The crowd gave a smattering of applause.

Wantoro was livid as he waited backstage. He held up a very firm finger, the muscles so tight it looked ready to break from his hand. "One day without nonsense, is all I ask!"

"He did a great job," said Raacyhila, twirling her red curls nervously. "He prepped for the role this whole season in fencing class and I really should have known he was feeling up to it. I just thought, with his episode at the choir performance…"

"Raaychila, don't. He can't continue to go off the rails like this. We should have sent him to Lejjone Panil years ago. Why have we waited this long?"

"He's got a month longer with us. Let's make it special."

"I want him out, tomorrow! He'll leave with the Nononias. It was Ms. Fritz's idea!" Wantoro huffed, cursed, and then sighed as he saw his son making his way to them. "Jeremy—"

Jeremy tossed Vordin Chikalto's helmet to Wantoro, who caught it with tense hands. Jeremy laughed. "Why would you start the reenactment without me? I was smooth though, right?" He patted his dad on the back. "I just improvised, you know, went with my gut." Jeremy was beaming now. "It's fine, everyone's talking about the smoke and the special effects, plus, let's be honest: I wore the helmet better."

Raaychila frowned. "Jeremy, go get ready for the dance."

"I look forward to it." Jeremy clapped and jogged away.

Raaychila crossed her arms and glanced at Wantoro, whose eyes were bulging. "Honey, it's okay, really. Be happy Jeremy's recovered from this morning's episode. I really thought that was going to ruin his whole day. He's building up resiliency, which you're always saying is so important."

"Just stop."

CHAPTER 5

THE EARTH STUDIES ACHIEVEMENT AWARD

The Watican Awards Ceremony's final event was nearing. Inside the Watican Hall, the guests were waiting for Jeremy and Maren to take the stage. Maren's parents, Mateo and Gillian, sat at a table next to a flower garden. Songbirds twittered in a bamboo cage, and Mateo whistled at them while Gillian fixed her makeup. Mateo pointed at the guards in white uniforms lining the perimeter of the hall.

"Look, Gillian! It's the Intergalactic Intelligence Unit. My uncle's wife's brother was a member, top secret stuff!" Mateo shoveled ginger biscuits into his mouth, then dusted off the crumbs. "You know," he added, "aside from the pomp and circumstance, I bet they're here on a mission. Maybe there's intelligence of a bomb scare! Remember a couple of years ago when–"

"Mateo, you're acting like a child! Put those cookies away." Gillian, a tall, bony woman with sharp cheek bones grabbed the package of cookies from Mateo and shoved them in her purse. "Our daughter will be up on that stage in a matter of minutes and I don't think it's appropriate to contemplate a bomb scare."

"I was only kidding. Have a drink." Mateo pointed to the cocktail in Gillian's hand and smiled.

"Mateo, Gillian." A squat woman with a severe bun pulled a chair up to Gillian and Mateo's table. She bowed before taking her seat.

"Ah, Ms. Fritz, one of the few Earth Scholars who've actually been to Earth! Lends credibility, am I right?" Mateo laughed.

"The pleasure's all mine. The journey wouldn't have been possible without your family's generous foundation." Ms. Fritz grinned and then helped herself to the ice box on the center of the table, taking an ice cube and generously slathering it onto her head in an attempt to slick illusionary stray hairs back onto her scalp.

Gillian watched this with contempt, but tried her best to mask her judgment. "Ms. Fritz, I'm told you might be accompanying Maren and Jeremy to Lejjone Panil Boarding School?"

"Yes, Ms. Nononia. Jeremy doesn't know, but his parents will break the news at breakfast tomorrow. They thought it best not to rock the boat tonight, in case… well, you know." Ms. Fritz made the sign for insanity with her finger.

Gillian cringed at her trespass.

The blue light from the chandeliers dimmed and a hush went over the songbirds. Mateo gave a descending "wooooooooooo!" for good measure.

"Oh, look! Here they come!" Gillian raised her hand to her mouth as Maren entered onto the stage, her hair swept into a twist, a single curl at the nape of her neck. She wore a pink silk leotard and matching tu-tu, with lace frill accenting her sleeves. Maren's silver slippers padded across the stage, an 'aw!' from the audience meeting her halfway. The audience applauded as she arched onto her tippy toes and twinkled across the stage, her arms curved above her head.

Jeremy entered right in a gold leotard speckled with silver clocks. He smiled his most angelic smile, his bright white teeth glistening, and kicked up his legs to a crescendo championed by the orchestra pit. After he nailed the landing, he twirled tantalizingly close to Maren. The audience gasped and applauded.

After a few more moves, Maren leapt into the air and Jeremy caught her by the waist. He raised her up while they circled the stage. He placed her down, and it was time for Maren's solo. She leapt around the stage and finished with a triple twirl. Maren and Jeremy bowed to thunderous applause.

Maren was told that after her triple twirl, she'd bow, the lights would dim, and she'd exit left before Jeremy's solo. Instead, he took her hand, leaned in and whispered, "We weave our story through the language of movement." Whatever *that* means. The orchestra struck up again, and he pulled her back center stage with him, caressing her hand before bringing it down to her side. She stilled as he ran right of center, leapt and executed a quadruple twirl. Then drawing near her once more, he extended his leg straight and arched his body in a flawless line, and balanced there, a living sculpture of strength and beauty. He spoke in a low voice, "Listen: you're dignified, a silhouette of quiet intensity." Jeremy leapt from his position to a roll, then sprung up, higher still, defying gravity, then—each rotation of his body faster than the last, his foot whipping the air as he pivoted on pointe. As the music reached its crescendo, he landed with a flourish beside Maren as the audience roared.

When the performance concluded, Maren and Jeremy bowed demurely and waved. The conductor gestured to them. "Thank you, Cajjez Jeremy Chikalto and Maren Nononia, for that innovative performance of *The Battle of Bhan Plateau*. And now it is with great honor that I introduce Vinya Raaychila Chikalto."

Jeremy and Maren ran off stage, tucking themselves gingerly into the club box.

Raaychila entered onto the stage and bowed, thanking the conductor as she took the microphone. "On behalf of the board of the Nononia Earth Studies Foundation I welcome all of you, and I thank you for extending a heartfelt Watican welcome to our special guests.

"Two-hundred years ago," continued Raaychila, "We inaugurated the Earth Studies Achievement Award to keep faith with an idea. The people of our galaxy, though separated from Earth, can still achieve enlightenment with our Earthen kin.

"The nominees for this year's Earth Studies Achievement Award: Lilith Pendoza, Senior Technical Analyst of the Watican Royal Guard, who deciphered an Earthen global satellite system code; Gorda Fritz, Earth Studies Scholar and leader of the Milky Way Geological Research Group, whose work on volcanism and deep seismic-reflection expanded our understanding of Earth's surface; and Peter Nebolt, Professor of Religious Studies at Bester University, for his work on the Qumran Scrolls and analysis of archeological data on the site of discovery." Raaychila took a deep breath and peered over the audience. "And the Earth Studies Achievement Award goes to... Ms. Gorda Fritz, Earth Studies Scholar and leader of the Milky Way Geological Research Team."

Gorda Fritz slathered another ice cube onto her head before rising from her seat.

The audience applauded as she made her way to the stage. "Thank you," said Ms. Fritz, taking the microphone and holding the award up over her head. "It is with a profound sense of humility that I accept this award. The journey to and from Earth is long and trying: five years to arrive on Earth's atmosphere thanks to advancements in beam technology, but a harrowing twenty-year return journey. Not many before myself have chosen to make it. It's a sacrifice, and one must learn to let go of her ties to the Farmoore Galaxy. I was fortunate to travel with my parents, both scientists before me, and I think that they are truly the ones who deserve this award, God rest their souls. Earth is a planet of rich volcanic activity. In the Farmoore Galaxy, not one of our planets has ever had a single volcanic eruption, and I tell you, it is an awesome force of nature." Ms. Fritz's eyes glazed over with tears. "The Mantel, especially, is a beautiful and highly viscous layer."

CHAPTER 6

A VISIT FROM BEYOND

After Ms. Fritz had finished her speech and Raaychila made her closing remarks, Jeremy began to prematurely take off his ballet costume, walking off backstage with his chest exposed in a fit of laughter. "The Mantel, especially, is a beautiful and highly viscous layer!" he cried out between laughs. Maren watched as the heavy gold-plated doors swung behind him. She smiled in spite of herself.

Maren changed and then joined her parents at their table. She took a seat and picked through her father's dessert plate for a pastry puff.

"That was just a breathtaking performance, Maren," cooed Gillian. "So much more mature than I was ready for, really, but so elegant—the way you carried yourself up there."

"It was nice, but I could do with less hand holding," said Mateo.

"Mateo! It's ballet! It's supposed to look romantic!" Gillian slapped at Mateo's arm. "So Maren, what do you think of Jeremy since you last saw him?"

"Oh," Maren set down her pastry.

"He's handsome, right?" pressed Gillian.

"Mom!"

"Well of course he is," said Gillian. "Mateo, do you think they would make a good match? I've been torn about this for years now. He was such a child before, but this year! His voice is lower. He's strong. It's all happening, hmm?"

"Hah!" was all Mateo managed to say.

"Years?" Maren frowned.

"Oh honey, don't be naive. You're destined to marry someone powerful and well-connected. And he's the Cajjez! The Vinya likes you. They're watching and everyone's still so young, so we're cautious, of course. But these moments could lay the foundation for something to come. I know they just had the Famtuan's in from Andacian, and their daughter is the same age, but Maren, you're so smart and–"

"Dependable, reliable, they need that for him," said Mateo matter-of-factly. "But if you don't like him, you tell your mom to eat grass. You're all too young anyway." He waved them off.

"Of course Jeremy's behavior is a bit disturbing, and he's so arrogant. But I can't help to wonder. Maybe he's matured a lot since our last visit? Anyway, I think you'll find out soon enough." Gillian smiled ear to ear, an in-the-know tell for her.

Maren hushed her mom and looked around sheepishly. "I don't think so. I'm going to bed."

Jeremy leaned over his bed and clicked off his bedside lamp. The light dimmed until the room was pitch black. A gentle breeze came in from his window in the spire. He pulled the covers tighter around him. "I think things are okay between me and Maren, Lyrna. I hope I can talk to her more tomorrow. She looked great up there on the stage. Poised, confident. But she probably didn't want me coaching her. She hates me, right? Sometimes I think she likes me."

Lyrna settled at the foot of his bed, her long ear tufts bobbing up and down as she groomed herself. She grunted.

Something fell off Jeremy's dresser and crashed to the floor. Lyrna hissed and slinked under the bed.

"Lyrna, come back!" Jeremy sighed and fluffed his pillow. He stared up at the high vaulted ceilings, recalling in his mind's eye Maren's open-backed dress, the way it draped her figure in pink silk, her lustrous blonde hair piled on top of her head, her pouty lips… *Maybe I shouldn't think about her like that. I'm too impulsive. It's problematic.*

CRACK.

Jeremy's heart jumped and he sat up in bed. Moonlight filtered in through his windows, casting strange shadows on his walls. The room was buzzing as though every object was vibrating subtly together.

CRACK.

"Lyrna?" But Jeremy knew it wasn't Lyrna. The air began to twitch.

"It's happening again. Hey Lyrna, come here?" Jeremy's pulse quickened. "Please?" He patted his covers. "Lyrna?"

"Jer–" A deep, hollow voice reverberated in the air.

A voice! That was new. Definitely new. "Hello?" Jeremy's voice trailed off.

CRACK.

It was the loudest crack yet. Jeremy felt a tug at his insides. He sensed that if he wanted to, he could leave his room entirely and go behind the air.

"Jeremy Chikalto," said the voice.

He faced the source of the voice. There, in the center of the room, floated a wispy mass. It was faintly human. Its long face would materialize every few seconds, revealing shades of purple. Pieces of hair floated in and out of space, undulating like snakes.

Jeremy opened his mouth to speak, but found that he could not.

"Jeremy Chikalto," said the voice. "The end comes for you."

Jeremy gazed into the void of the creature's eyes. "What... what are you?"

"I am of another essence, sent to..." The messenger disappeared. Jeremy kicked the covers off his legs and moved closer to the source of the voice. He could feel his night clothes move with a magnetic tide, pulling in and out. The messenger reappeared in front of him and he stumbled back, almost falling over the chest at the foot of his bed.

"...sevenfold." The messenger fizzled slightly. "You are meant for this space... come through the Haze." The messenger disappeared.

CRACK.

Jeremy held his breath and waved his hand over the area where the presence had been. Nothing. He crawled along the floor, looking for some sign, some tangible pile of ash, singed fabric, drops of liquid. Still nothing. A breeze rustled his curtain and he ran to the window, breathing in the fresh air. Jeremy looked up at the night sky and felt a sense of urgency overtake him. Was it a dream? Some part of him always knew he'd receive a visitor from beyond.

CHAPTER 7

LEJJONE PANIL

The morning after the Awards Ceremony, the Nononias and Ms. Fritz accompanied the Chikaltos to the race track. Wantoro, Gillian, Mateo, Maren and Ms. Fritz sat at a table in a skybox overlooking the pill-shaped track, a royal breakfast spread before them. The crowd below chattered as the horses and jockeys lined up. Gillian frowned as she extracted an orange petal from her morning cocktail. The door to the skybox swung open and Jeremy walked in slowly, with Raaychila guiding him from behind with her hands on his shoulders.

"Here come the horses! Oh, I mean…" Mateo pointed at Raaychila and Jeremy, the dimples in his red apple cheeks pulsating as he slapped his knee.

"Jeremy, you're looking so lively this morning," said Vor Wantoro as his son appeared. "What's this? Freshen up some."

Jeremy's hair was bedraggled and his eyes were puffy. He didn't acknowledge Wantoro, and slumped into his chair.

"Yes, let's just proceed." Raaychila forced a smile as she took her seat. She shuffled through her purse and set a small pile of pills beside Jeremy's water glass.

A gun fired and the horses took off. Mateo let out a squeal. "Our bet's on Diamond in the Rough, right Maren?"

Maren smiled, glanced at Jeremy, then looked back at the racetrack. The horses rounded the first bend.

Jeremy lifted each pill that his mother had given him. "Anti-psychotic, anxiety, mood stabilizer, no, no, and no." He pushed the pills away from him.

Raaychila fanned herself and looked around to make sure no one heard him.

Vor Wantoro cleared his throat and then lifted his glass. "Congratulations to Ms. Gorda Fritz for her award. I know we've talked in private about—"

"Boarding school, yes," interrupted Ms. Fritz. "And I will be honored to oversee his studies, beginning," she turned to Jeremy, "tomorrow."

"Wantoro, maybe stick to the original plan, he leaves in a month?" Raaychila patted the back of Jeremy's seat. "He's not well."

"Is that the polite way of saying I'm crazy?" Jeremy's sapphire eyes flashed tempestously and then he slipped back into his revelry. *The end comes. Travel to the Haze. Sevenfold.* Jeremy pulled the nearest plate of pancakes and bacon across the table and began heaping generous portions onto his plate.

Ms. Fritz lifted an eyebrow.

"There goes our horse!" Mateo said weakly.

Maren shifted uncomfortably, her attentions divided.

Wantoro drummed his hand on the table in front of Jeremy, who seemed unresponsive. "Jeremy, how would you feel about going to boarding school tomorrow, with Ms. Fritz and the Nononias? It'll be good for you. No need to wait a month."

"Jeremy?" whispered Maren.

"Maybe we should just leave him alone, he's not feeling well," said Raaychila.

"I think I need to share something," blurted Jeremy.

Ms. Fritz leaned forward across the table. "Forgive me, Vor Wantoro, if I speak out of place, but I don't think he should be entertaining options. His education can begin today, really, with you holding firm your decision to send him to Lejjone Panil tomorrow." She set her mouth in a tight line.

Vor Wantoro reclined in his seat and smirked. "That's a very bold statement to make, Ms. Fritz. What I'm to do with *my* son."

"Excuse me?" Jeremy stood up and jostled the table, knocking Maren's plate to the floor. It shattered by Maren's feet. "I think I may be... well, Vordin Chikalto is our bloodline, so, and I think you need to listen to me. It could be, oh the divine um, reawake, reawakening, something celestial."

"Jeremy, sit down!" said Wantoro. "Raaychila, take him away!"

"I've told you about the air and there's something behind it," continued Jeremy. "I know you think I'm crazy, ill, er migraines," he looked briefly at Maren. "It came to me! Last night, there was a creature, like a ghost. I was told the end is coming. We've been taught to honor Vordin Chikalto's legacy—our family's legacy—the mistakes on the battlefield. We have to prepare."

"Who told you this?"

"Raaychila!" said Wantoro sternly.

"I was visited by a, by a ghost, an angel!"

Wantoro stood up and pulled his son by the arm, dragging him across the booth. "I'm sorry. My son's brain is in space, as they say."

Maren rose from her seat and stood warily behind her parents.

Ms. Fritz called after Wantoro, "Send your son to Lejjone Panil tomorrow! I will help him. There is no judgment here!"

The Cajjez bucked and contorted as Wantoro pulled him down the stairs, guards closing in around them, and back out to an armored vehicle. His father crammed him into the back seat, then made for the front. Jeremy yelled, "An angel visited me last night! An angel!" The armored vehicle took off with its motorcade.

Jeremy's father had him sequestered on the tenth floor of the castle. Guards were posted at the exits. Jeremy paced the hallway. He'd acted recklessly. "The end is coming," he said under his breath. "*That* wasn't the way to handle it."

Jeremy closed his eyes and took a deep breath. Someone had turned the corner and was heading down the hallway.

"Jeremy," said Ms. Fritz, her arm outstretched in preparation for a handshake. It seemed unnecessary to initiate a handshake from such a distance.

"What do you want?" Jeremy rubbed his temples, deciding it best to occupy his hands and so avoid the pending handshake altogether. Who was this random woman, really, inserting herself at such a delicate time. He knew she won the award, but could care less.

"My apologies. I'm Gorda Fritz, Earth Scholar and now it seems, your personal mentor. I am to accompany you to Lejjone Panil." Ms. Fritz stood in front of the Cajjez, her hand still awkwardly extended. Jeremy turned his back on her.

"Right. School. Very important, sure, sure." He turned to her. "Listen. I don't care for you or for going to school. It's like, really insignificant right now, and I have tutors here. We don't need to talk about that. And you should know," he continued, "that I really did see a spirit."

"I know," said Ms. Fritz.

Jeremy stepped back, almost losing his balance. "What? How do you know?" He studied her with an air of suspicion. Was this some attempt to manipulate him? Who had sent her?

"I know because I've been contacted by a spirit myself. Now, I've been angling to have a private word with you for some time. You mustn't mention this to your parents. They have agreed to let you study under me. But please, no more talk of this spirit or angel. We must leave soon." Ms. Fritz slicked her hair down with her stocky hand. She adjusted her glasses and leaned forward.

Jeremy eyed her. "Why you?"

"Because my purpose is to guide you. To... introduce you to a powerful friend of mine. I need to see you off this planet. You must come with me to Lejjone Panil tomorrow."

Jeremy looked up at the white marble ceiling. His eyes traced the swirls of gray, which looked like tempestuous clouds, as though a storm were gathering overhead. The angel *had* mentioned that he should leave and travel to the Haze. "Ms. Fritz," said Jeremy. It was against his better judgment, but he was desperate for answers. Maybe she had something useful to teach him after all. "I believe you. I'll leave tomorrow."

CHAPTER 8

THE JOURNEY BEGINS

All of Jeremy's most prized possessions lay stacked before the elevator doorway. In choosing what to bring to boarding school and what to leave behind, he erred on the side of inclusion, and selected, among other things, his entire wardrobe, all of his instruments and paintings, and half of his music library.

Castle staff carried heaps up the walkway into the Nononias' spaceship parked on the castle's landing strip. The ship was Mateo's pride and joy, with a smooth, semicircle body resting on cylinders housing the engines, which now hummed gently. Maren was both annoyed and amused as the cargo space of their ship was overtaken by the Cajjez's essentials.

It was midday and galanbirds flitted overhead, casting shadows through the skylights of the castle's west wing. Raaychila followed Jeremy into his room.

"And you'll make friends! You can write to me about the air and about your meditation. I just wouldn't lead with that, with friends and all."

"Is this necessary?" said Wantoro from outside the bedroom. He was standing in front of the elevator and staring with disdain at the mountains of suitcases and Lyrna gear.

Raaychila surveyed Jeremy's bedroom. "Did you pack your medicine? You have to take it three times a day."

"Yep," Jeremy lied.

"We'll be in contact with your care team. You aren't escaping this. If you experience something while you're away that frightens you, anything, I want to be the first person you tell. We'll laugh it away."

"That sounds insensitive, but okay." Jeremy shook his head and emptied his arms of lotions, powders, and scented oils into a bag.

Wantoro observed the pile's contents. "No, no. Don't bring any of that stuff. When you're out of this castle, you're to seem less high maintenance. You need to be a man of the people, not some pampered, puffed-up–"

"Dad, hi? Pampered, puffed up? I can throw a ball just as well as a kick. Such a tender goodbye for your only son."

Raaychila wrapped her arms around Jeremy and kissed his cheek. She caught a whiff of mint and eucalyptus. "Okay, maybe you should leave the scented oils behind." She grabbed the bag of oils and started to put it in her purse.

"Hey, I have lavender in there. It's calming. It helps, it does." Jeremy smiled, swiped the bag back, fished out the lavender and then tore the lid off. He dumped it on the floor, shaking the bottle to get out every last drop. "There, something to remember me by, Father. Olfactory senses make for strong memories." He tossed the bottle, relishing the crazed look in his father's eyes.

"I wish you hadn't done that." Raaychila motioned for a butler to clean up the offending odor. "Remember, be approachable and warm. Kind and careful."

"And a lot less impulsive," said Wantoro.

Jeremy waved them off. "Sure, sure. Love you both! See you soon!"

Jeremy boarded the spaceship with Maren. Since the school Lejjone Panil was close to the planet Olg, he would travel with the Nononias. Ms. Fritz also boarded the spaceship. She promised Wantoro and Raaychila that she'd keep an eye on Jeremy and help him with his studies, enlisting a team of top-rated therapists for support.

Inside the spaceship, the walls were decorated with a pattern of endless knots woven with cobalt blue and soft gold. Jeremy sat on the corner couch and rested his head on a yellow needlepoint pillow. Lyrna meowed from her carrier, a silver crate adorned with precious stones.

Maren sat on a couch opposite Jeremy. "Do you want to listen to The Moonstones or Velvet Tiger? Or just, like, talk radio?" She fiddled with her tablet and the wall speakers powered up.

"Whichever," said Jeremy.

"Okay, I'll just do The Moonstones." She hesitated, then tapped her tablet, and gentle synth ambience filled the room.

Ms. Fritz burst in and walked over to Jeremy's couch. Jeremy glared at her, but she took no notice and sat next to Lyrna's cage. She tapped it with her walking stick and Lyrna growled.

"She's a sentient being so don't tap her carrier like she's some rodent." Jeremy leaned back on the sofa and crossed his arms. Ms. Fritz might be an ally, but he still regarded her as subordinate. He'd make her go away. "Ms. Fritz," said Jeremy. "Release Lyrna from her cage."

"Absolutely not. It's unsanitary—we're about to eat."

Lyrna growled. "Bad lady."

"Watch how you talk about my fizdruft, Gorda." Jeremy walked to Lyrna's cage and released her. As he was about to take his seat, Ms. Fritz hobbled up from behind him and grabbed Lyrna by the scruff of the neck. Maren gasped.

It was too late. Lyrna twisted her body around and bared her teeth, each roughly the size of Ms. Fritz's thumb. She batted her arms and sank her claws into Ms. Fritz's neck. The stout woman screamed and threw Lyrna, who didn't retract her claws and instead took chunks of Ms. Fritz's flesh with her. Blood splattered onto the carpet and Lyrna ran under Jeremy's sofa.

"You're lucky," said Jeremy.

While Ms. Fritz was moaning and covering her gushing wounds with her hands, Mateo, Maren, and two spaceship personnel ran to get the medic. Jeremy trotted to the beat of the synths and then picked Lyrna up by the ear tuft, scooped up her bottom, and walked to the kitchen.

When Ms. Fritz's wounds were bandaged and the carpets and upholstery cleaned, Maren excused herself to find Jeremy.

The lights were dim. Maren approached the back of a wide, cushioned chair and saw the bobbing of golden brown hair. She moved cautiously towards him, anticipating yet another failed exchange.

"Hey Maren," he said calmly. Maren approached his side. He was eating bits of fruit, nuts, and cheese from a spread on the glass countertop. Lyrna crouched beside the plate, nibbling at a smaller pile.

"Hi." Maren tucked her hair behind her ears. "I can't believe Ms. Fritz did that. Doesn't she know about fizdrufts?"

"I guess not. Some scholar, eh? Have a seat." Jeremy gestured. Startled, Maren looked around her. There was no additional seating at his end of the counter.

"I'll just stand." Her pulse quickened. Lyrna looked up from her snack.

"We could be talking for a while. Sit here, with me." Jeremy slid to the right, allowing just enough space for Maren to squeeze beside him. "Big chairs. We can handle this."

Maren wavered, then tucked in beside him. It didn't have to be a big deal if she didn't make it a big deal.

"Ms. Fritz, what an idiot. I can't imagine her overseeing my studies," said Jeremy, rolling his eyes. "She's one of those petty tyrants–hey don't look at me like that, I'd never be a petty tyrant."

"You told her to unlock Lyrna's cage," said Maren. "You could have unlocked it yourself, she's your pet." She immediately regretted sharing the chair with him.

"That's not 'petty tyrant' level behavior." Jeremy crossed his arms.

"I don't know, just something to think about." Maren sighed. Even through her sleeve, she kept rubbing against his arm. What if she fell into him? "Anyway, you might have to get used to taking some direction from time to time, even if you don't agree with it. Teachers aren't always a good fit, but you just learn to defer to them, choose your battles wisely. I can tell you about Lejjone Panil, if you'd like?" She looked at her lap.

"Well, I'm going to be straight with you. That sounds boring."

Maren let out a small laugh, "Well, it'll be a lot to take in, and not just new teachers, but your schedule will—"

"I'm already bored." Jeremy held his hand up in protest. "We could talk about our dance."

"Oh that, right," Maren laughed again and hated herself for it. It was a fake, nervous laugh. "I think *The Battle of Bhan Plateau* was a huge success. I'm so glad it worked out with us, you know, not practicing together. We didn't need to, I mean."

"You did great. You really held yourself with such grace, Maren."

"Thank you. And you, well, that was lovely, lovely as always." Maren smiled, then reached for cheese and crackers.

"You think I was lovely?" Jeremy cocked his head to the side, bemused. "I would have liked to hear strong, or maybe some compliment about my artistry or athleticism."

"You don't get to choose which compliments you receive."

"You just," Jeremy massaged his temples, "you never give me what I want."

"Careful," said Maren, standing up. "Take care of your words, Cajjez. Words make a man's character. Actions make a man's character."

"Well then, what's this mean." Jeremy stood up, faced Maren, flexed his index finger and gave her a pronounced flick on the forehead. She started backwards, nearly falling.

"Stop," he laughed, "you're overreacting with that!"

"Real mature. What a charmer." Maren covered her forehead and made for the living room.

"Come on, it was a joke."

"You respect other people and their space!" she spit back at him before disappearing around the corner.

"I respect other people and their space?" he called back to her. "Well, that sounds like the right thing to me. Hey Lyrna, did she say it wrong? Is it just me? She said I respect other people and their space, like it's a bad thing."

"Instruct," said Lyrna.

"Right, instruction, sure. Well, I think she just got confused. Flicked her too hard in the head," Jeremy laughed to himself, frowned, then slammed his fist on the counter. Lyrna hissed.

CHAPTER 9

MS. FRITZ'S PLAN

Six days passed on the spaceship, and Mateo was trying in vain to ration the meats, cakes, and fine cheeses, with Gillian's stock of cocktail umbrellas all but exhausted. Jeremy had taken over the reading room of the spaceship, and while the ship belonged to the Nononias, Jeremy's moodiness and fits and starts with Maren so irked Gillian that she let him have his way, insisting that his reformation could only happen at Lejjone Panil.

Ms. Fritz knocked on the door to Gillian and Mateo's living quarters. Maren opened it and Ms. Fritz barreled past her, bumping the tea table. "Hello, sorry!" she panted as she stabilized the teetering cups. "It struck me as absurd that Jeremy and I should have our little standoff. He's haughty and ill-tempered but I should have known about the dangers of improperly handling a fizdruft."

Maren waivered in the doorway. "Should I go?"

"Nonsense," said Gillian. "Have a seat, Maren, Ms. Fritz." She gestured to Ms. Fritz to continue. "You were saying?"

"I'd like to treat the Cajjez to a meal on one of Failrun's moons. I hear Bexin's Restaurant on Findle is excellent." Ms. Fritz's hands trembled as she placed them behind her back.

Gillian exchanged glances with Mateo, who grumbled and busied himself with his eggs. Gillian sipped her tea and examined Gorda Fritz. The woman still wore her curling cap and her head kept wobbling back and forth. "Coffee, Ms. Fritz?" said Gillian.

Ms. Fritz quickly accepted.

But neither Gillian nor Mateo moved, so Maren made herself helpful and poured a cup of coffee for Ms. Fritz.

"Thank you, dear," said Ms. Fritz. She sipped her coffee to fill the dead air. "We'll be in Findle's orbit within the hour, so shall I tell Jeremy?"

Gillian frowned. "Yes, fine. We could all use some fresh air."

Jeremy sat cross-legged on the hardwood floor of the spaceship's reading room, his hands resting on his lap. A flame flickered before him, dancing on a gold candle set in a silver dish. Jeremy concentrated on his breath, alternating in time with the fluctuations of the candle's heat. Then: Foreground. Background. Eyes open. Shut. It was one way of exploring the place behind the air. Jeremy found that he could will the air to tremble. Once or twice, he dared to put his hand behind it. The door creaked open.

"Hello Jeremy," said Ms. Fritz.

Jeremy's body shook, and his two worlds fused back together. "I was meditating. I hate interruptions." Jeremy swished his hand in dismissal. He closed his eyes, intent on beginning the process over again.

"Cajjez, I am sorry about our—"

"Really? You're going to be that way?" Jeremy leaned forward and blew out the flame. "There. Go on. Is your hand okay? Did you read up on fizrufts?" He jabbed his finger at the shelf to his left. "Second shelf down from the top, third book in. Book on fizdrufts. You're welcome. But whatever, go on."

Ms. Fritz looked confused but then continued.

"Cajjez, do you know what they call Earth's interior?"

"I have no intention of becoming an Earth Studies scholar."

"Most of Earth's mass is in the mantel."

"Fascinating." Jeremy sighed. "Great talk."

"Yes, Mantel. Jeremy, have you ever thought that maybe there could be a third entity vying for power over the souls of man? God, Lucifer, and then—"

"What exactly do you want?"

Ms. Fritz adjusted her glasses and moved towards Jeremy, who felt violated by her proximity in this small room. Both her distressed demeanor and her plastic, pink cap distracted the Cajjez.

"Is that a shower cap? What is that on your head?" This detail consumed him.

"Oh! I'm just setting my curls. Never mind it. Anyway, we had a most unfortunate encounter earlier in the week." Ms. Fritz pointed to the bandage on her neck. "I want to start over again. I've arranged–"

Jeremy jumped to his feet. "You're tutoring me, the Cajjez, with that thing in your hair?" Jeremy laughed and circled Ms. Fritz. "I'll be distracted and hard to reach. Now, I can lack a sense of self-awareness at times, so I'll give you a free pass if you feel you truly need it on your head."

Ms. Fritz felt self-conscious. Her shoulders hunched forward and she warped back to elementary school. To her left sat Kendra Dondi, the most popular girl in school. Kendra was giggling incessantly, crying out, "Gorda Fritz is a dog! Gorda Fritz is an ugly, frizzy-haired dog!" The other students laughed. Petan Smitt, Gorda's elementary school crush, shot a spitball. It landed splat in Gorda's hair.

Jeremy was staring at Ms. Fritz. "Please continue and tell me what was so important that you forgot to take off your shower cap? I'm intrigued now."

"Oh, oh, yes!" Ms. Fritz's sagging posture snapped back into its rigid position. "Jeremy, Cajjez, I would like to treat you to a meal on one of Failrun's moons. To be honest, I feel awful about what happened and want to make amends."

"Don't ever insult my fizdruft again."

"Yes, of course. So how about it? A meal on Findle?"

Jeremy folded his hands in his lap. "I'll go if Maren and Lyrna can come along. Me and you can talk about our... spirit meetings. But I'd like a moment alone with Maren. If I ask her, she'll say no. I'm trying to be less neurotic about getting my way." He hesitated. "I mean, we're negotiating here, so I'm actively trying to get what I want from you. But it's different with her. Am I making sense? I'll go with you if Lyrna and Maren join me."

Ms. Fritz's mouth was set in a grim line. "Y...es. Yes, all right. I'll treat them too. I would have preferred just the two of us, but I can arrange for you young people to... flirt." Gorda scratched at the wound on her neck and a small spot of blood bloomed through her bandage.

Jeremy cringed. How could *this* lady teach him anything?

The spaceship touched ground on Findle, the largest of Failrun's three moons.

"Gorda?" said Gillian. She slurped the last of her cranberry cocktail through a red straw. "Assemble some guards to accompany you and the kids."

Gorda looked out the window at the tall trees swaying in the wind, the faint outline of another moon cresting in the pink sky. "Of course. Why don't you all go on outside and relax. I'll be right out." She flinched and drummed her fingers on the window sill.

Jeremy and Maren stepped outside the spaceship's front doors and into the chilly air. They walked over to a docking bay pavilion beside the spaceship and sat down.

"Isn't it beautiful?" said Maren, pointing to the sky.

"Yes, it is," said Jeremy, glancing up momentarily.

"Going to boarding school is a pretty big deal for you. Have you ever been separated from your family? From the castle?"

"I have not," said Jeremy with a sigh. "But, I mean, the castle is so big, I've gone days without seeing them."

Maren frowned.

Jeremy sat up a little taller. "This is fine. I'm so happy for the space, you know? I mean, you must know. Your mom is incredibly overbearing."

"Hey! Don't deflect. We're talking about *you*, Cajjez."

Jeremy smiled and looked at his lap. "You don't have to call me that, you know. I don't think I like it."

"How can you not like it? It's part of your identity. And it'll change soon. Someday you'll be Vor." Maren bit her lip.

"I don't know. That's not… a given, right? A given right, double entendre." He laughed.

"You're pretty clever, too," said Maren.

"Are you having an inner dialogue with yourself? I'm clever, but I'm also something else? Or, am I clever like you're clever? You are, by the way. Clever. My parents won't stop reminding me. And of course, I recognize it."

A gust of wind kicked up. A small, white spaceship hovered over the lot beside the Nononia's before landing softly.

"Maren! Do you see that?" Mateo came running to the pavilion. "It's an Intergalactic Intelligence Craft! Wonder what it's doing here. I saw some members of the IIU back on Watico, but didn't have a chance to talk. I'm going to round up some attendants for an official greeting! Jeremy, they'll stop for you—go say hi!" Mateo jogged into his own spaceship.

Jeremy and Maren stood up from the pavilion and walked over to the IIU ship. Jeremy desperately wanted to keep talking to Maren. He had so much to say, though he didn't know what he meant to say. Then it dawned on him that in leaving off the conversation, he didn't screw up. He didn't say or do the wrong thing, and this feeling of peace and stability blanketed him. *I want to savor this feeling.* And the warmth spread to his chest and played on his heart.

Two gentlemen and a stately lady descended from the craft's ramp. They wore crisp, white jumpsuits with red trim along the lapel and cuffs. On the breast pocket was embroidered a red flame inside a black circle—the symbol of the Intergalactic Intelligence Unit. The lady stepped forward and bowed.

"Cajjez Jeremy, sir, what an honor. And it is a pleasure to run into the esteemed Nononia family, as well."

Gillian and Mateo joined them, the latter grinning like a fanboy. "Yes, yes. Please join us for some refreshments," said Mateo.

Jeremy nodded, still in his daze. "Nice to meet you."

The officers introduced themselves as Special Unit 64. The woman was Jasmine Diggs. She had radiant brown skin and wore her hair in a braided bun. The burly albino was Drew Meltivor. Then a man whom Jeremy recognized from the Watican Awards Ceremony leaned forward and shook their hands. "I'm Bentley Stinger, Intergalactic Intelligence High General," he said in a tense voice. Bentley's face was sharp and his brow arched low. "We'll have a drink, but then we must be going, with all respect. We're heading to the Consternium Shoppes, just a routine patrolling."

Ms. Fritz burst through the Nononia's spaceship door. "And look! What a coincidence."

Startled, Gillian turned towards Ms. Fritz. "What is it?"

Ms. Fritz leaned against the spaceship's landing gear, catching her breath. "We're heading to the Consternium Shoppes too. Would you be willing to accompany myself, the Cajjez and Maren?"

Gillian's cheeks flushed. "No, that's not necessary, we have our own guards."

"Of course," said Bentley quickly.

"But you have your official business—"

"As I said, we're just on patrol. We'll gladly accompany the Cajjez, Maren, and Ms. Fritz to their destination and back."

Mateo shrugged. "Well, the IIU is the best of the best."

CHAPTER 10

THE HAZE

Jeremy carried Lyrna in his arms. The pink sky cast an eerie light on Findle's docking bay, which stood at the center of an abstern forest. Large, knobby trees twisted around each other, their black bark mottled with slimy moss.

"Come along then. This way." Ms. Fritz led them along a forest path, their feet crunching on abstern mulch. The Intergalactic Intelligence Unit followed close behind. Bright fluorescent signs displayed ads on either side of the path:

"Jan's Petite Wear, mile marker 57!"
"Consternium Shoppes, mile marker 59!"
"Freeway Ground Transport, next right!"

Jeremy stroked Lyrna while she batted at a wave of hair on his forehead. He'd chance talking to her again. "I've never been to Findle. What language do they speak here?"

"Banstorm, mainly. But some people are fluent in English, too," said Maren.

"Banstorm." Jeremy considered this and decided that it might be amusing. "Let's stop at the shops and practice conversation. We can probably take the freeway ground transport up ahead." He had studied Banstorm up to the first year intermediate level, and though not fluent, Jeremy was certain his ability might impress Maren.

Maren was eager to agree on something. If the two were to spend a great deal of time together, they had better attempt to relate. "Okay, I'm sure my parents wouldn't mind if we're gone a little longer than expected. How many languages do you know, if you don't mind my asking?"

Ms. Fritz dropped back and walked beside Jeremy and Maren. "Nope! We're not going there. We're on a tight schedule."

"But I thought I heard my mom mention Bexin's Restaurant. Isn't that by the shoppes?" Maren faced the trail to the freeway ground transport, but Ms. Fritz and the IIU guards came behind Maren and Jeremy and guided them past it.

"Yes, well, no. See. Here. We keep walking." Ms. Fritz ushered them forward. "I wanted to go to a place that was close to the Consternium Shoppes, but not actually at it, if you understand me."

A branch pricked Jeremy's shoulder and he paused to rub it. "Fine by me," he said.

Maren looked quizzically at Jeremy.

Ms. Fritz pointed ahead and began striding faster. Her large, muscular legs rubbed together, the fabric chaffing her thighs.

"I'm fluent in two languages other than English: Medik and Canope. But I have a working ability in like, ten languages. Just basic level to dine with ambassadors. You?"

Marens smiled. "Ms. Fritz, so where exactly are we going?"

But Ms. Fritz only waddled up the path.

"English, Medik, Canope, same. I'm decent at Latin, I've been told," said Maren.

"Earth scholar track, right, I heard that about you. That's pretty cool. I know some translations for songs," he laughed, and he was embarrassed that he was acting so interested in Earth Studies after just disparaging it to Ms. Fritz.

At last, Ms. Fritz paused, and looked to her left. A lonely, narrow forest path rose sharply into the brambles. "This way!" said Ms. Fritz as she hurried up the path.

"Lyrna want toffee," said Lyrna.

Jeremy slowed and walked alongside Maren. Ms. Fritz's control of the party irked him and so he determined to counter her haste with his leisure. "El jut'uun frey sa'kla e tet?"

Maren smiled. He had good pronunciation and she didn't know why that surprised her. "Banecc frey e ver a'ste. Mejun no desun."

"Yum, sounds good. Refined," said Jeremy. "All the seasoning is done with local herbs. We could stop and collect some? I bet that's something." Maren and Jeremy stooped to grab a handful of plants on the side of the path. Maren started laughing.

The IIU stood and watched Maren and Jeremy with some amusement.

"Hurry along!" said Ms. Fritz, before disappearing around a shrub protruding across the trail.

While Jeremy and Maren pretended to be consumed by herb gathering, Ms. Fritz began to clear her throat over and over again. The sound was so annoying that they gave up and started walking again.

At last, Ms. Fritz came to a halt. Forty minutes had passed since they left the spaceship. One of the other Failrun moons, Sixi, was passing across the sun, and spread a shadow over the woods. Wind swept through the knotty trees and a dead, gnarled branch landed beside Jeremy's foot. He jumped back. "Ms. Fritz, where have you taken us? Why has it gone dark?"

Maren clapped her hands together. "Jeremy, lunar eclipses happen often on Findle. It should only last a couple of minutes. And because we're on a moon, you know, sometimes the planet Failrun even blocks out the sun and you can imagine how long the darkness lasts then!" But Jeremy's attention was on Ms. Fritz, who was slumped against a tree with a grotesque smile. Maren froze as she, too, took in Ms. Fritz's alarming countenance.

"Jeremy, you're not meant to go to Lejjone Panil," said Ms. Fritz.

Maren blinked. Jeremy was smiling too. Why was he smiling?

"Go on," said Jeremy.

"An angel wants to speak with you."

"Lyrna scared." Lyrna leapt into Maren's arms.

"Jeremy, the angel is behind the air and it tells me that you must go to it now. You'll hear it call to you once you're on the other side. Follow the call." Ms. Fritz's face was sallow. Beads of sweat stippled her cheeks and forehead.

"I don't know how–"

"Yes! Yes you do! The angel tells me that you do know how!" Ms. Fritz looked at Jeremy and then Maren. She scanned the forest for the IIU in vain. The darkness from the eclipse made it impossible to see anything beyond ten feet, the trees further limiting sight.

"I've never... I don't know," said Jeremy. How could he possibly just cross over? And why now?

"That's impossible. Of course you know!" Ms. Fritz shook her head in frustration. A cold wind gusted and another dead branch landed between Jeremy and Maren.

"I suppose..."

"Yes?" said Ms. Fritz.

Maren was growing faint. Still cradling Lyrna in one arm, she backed away and groped behind her for a tree. "Jeremy?"

Jeremy, distracted, ignored Maren and stepped forward. "I suppose I've almost crossed over before, but never completely. I get," he hesitated, "frightened. My chest—"

"Jeremy, what are you talking about?" Maren's mouth had gone to cotton.

"This doesn't concern you, Miss Nononia!" said Ms. Fritz. She beckoned Jeremy to come closer, and he did. Ms. Fritz smiled as she unveiled a dark purple orb from her pocket. Holding it to eye level, she whispered, "Mantel, letum libero everto."

Jeremy's heart was racing. "Maren? Are you seeing this?"

"You have to go behind the air to the Haze. Cajjez, try to listen to the voices," said Ms. Fritz.

"The Haze?" Jeremy's eyes widened. It had all happened so soon. "Can I come back? What is the Haze?"

Maren now crouched at the base of a tree. She stroked Lyrna's puffed fur and shivered. "Jeremy? I want to get out of here. I'm going to... go back to the ship now."

"No you're not, Maren! You stay right there!" Ms. Fritz glared at Maren and massaged the small orb, which was now emitting a high frequency hissing sound. "Jeremy, tell her to stay!"

"Stop shouting at her! Can't you see she's scared?" yelled Jeremy. "It's okay, Maren, you can stay here with me. You'll see." His voice wavered as he turned to face Maren and Lyrna. He could barely make out their outlines against the dark clutter of trees.

"Cajjez Jeremy. Listen to me. I don't want you to get distracted by your friends."

"But they know about the spirit already. Maren? I wanted you to see that it's the truth."

"I don't know, I just… Jeremy, I want to go home!" yelled Maren.

"Jeremy! Everyone will be all right, but in order for this very important thing to work…" Gorda Fritz stomped her foot three times on the ground. Her voice strained. "For this to work, I must have order!"

The shrubs behind Ms. Fritz began to sway. Twigs snapped.

"Maren Nononia," said Bentley, emerging behind Ms. Fritz.

"Yes?" Maren's eyes searched the darkness. She had forgotten about the IIU.

"Gorda, what should we do about Maren? This wasn't part of the plan."

Jeremy opened his mouth to speak but was cut off by Ms. Fritz.

"Someone detain her. Get her to calm down." Ms. Fritz held the orb to eye level. "Mantel, letum libero everto!"

Jeremy was beginning to lose faith in this grand scheme he knew nothing about. Why had Ms. Fritz lied to him about the restaurant? What did the angel want with him? Was it so important that he cross over right at this moment? He hardly felt ready. Jeremy glanced at Maren and Lyrna. Two figures now stood behind them, and the taller, albino man placed a hand on Maren's shoulder.

"Just relax," said Drew.

Maren shuddered under the weight of the foreign hand.

"Cajjez Jeremy," said Ms. Fritz, "you must cross over. You're the only one who can travel through the Haze. Never mind about your friends, we'll take good care of them for you. Seek out Mantel! He will tell you what to do next. Remember that."

Jeremy kept his eyes on Maren and Lyrna, both of whom were in shock. He could see them clearer now against the white uniforms of the IIU. He tried to concentrate on the subtle vibrations welling up in his sternum. "I can feel the sensation. I think I can do this."

"Ms. Fritz?" said the tall albino man, his hand resting on his holster, "Just give the order."

"Wait!" yelled Bentley, but it was too late. Jeremy saw the gun.

"Ms. Fritz! Why is his hand on the gun?" Jeremy moved towards Maren and Lyrna.

"It's nothing Jeremy! Now focus! And go to it!" Ms. Fritz flung the black orb onto the ground, closer to Jeremy. The orb screeched a dreadful sound that reverberated off the wall of trees. Ms. Fritz crouched low. "Go!"

"Gun?" It was all Maren could manage.

"Maren! Lyrna!" Jeremy reached out to them, grasping Maren's forearm and Lyrna's tail, and the vibrations in his chest erupted. His breath seemed to give way to a scream—only, the scream didn't belong to him. There was a jolt.

Everything flashed white and then purple. Jeremy blacked out for a moment and when he came to, his arms were wrapped around Maren's waist. Bentley also held Maren, only he had her in a stranglehold, his right arm pressed against her neck. Maren was still holding Lyrna, who hissed and sunk her claws and teeth into Bentley's arm. Bentley cried out and yanked his arm away. Maren stumbled forward.

The other two IIU members rushed over to restrain Lyrna. Ms. Fritz also grasped at Maren's shoulders, trying to wrestle her from Jeremy. The air around Jeremy twitched. When Ms. Fritz felt the field of static emitting from Jeremy, she pulled back and yelled, "Let them all go!" Bentley and the others withdrew. "Let them go to Mantel!"

Jeremy, his arms around Maren and Lyrna, felt a sharp tug on his sternum, and exhaled as Gorda Fritz and the Intergalactic Intelligence Unit blinked out of view.

Jeremy opened his eyes to another place. He was now behind the air and floating up through a wine-dark tunnel. Maren and Lyrna's eyes were closed, and their bodies were limp, bobbing along next to him. Jeremy carried them with ease as he swam to the bright light at the far end of the tunnel.

Aside from the bright light, the place was a hazy purple. The tunnel pulsated with static, and a magnetic force centered Jeremy in his ascent. *Have I died?* Jeremy turned away from the bright light and felt the sting of tears on his eyes and cheeks.

There was a scream. Then a hollow voice called out "Jeremy..."

"It's an angel! Maren, it's an angel!" Jeremy stopped floating up towards the light and shook Maren. He wanted her to see, to believe him. But Maren and Lyrna were asleep. Maren was draining of color, and she drew labored breaths.

"Jer... Come this way!" said a woman's voice, taking the place of the first.

***

Bloody heads littered the forest floor at the base of a mountain. Twenty cloaked disciples circled an executioner, who pushed a headless corpse, still convulsing, to the ground. Another disciple stepped forward, and the executioner threw her body on a stone slab, her chin cracking on the rock. "For Mantel. Mantel, letum libero everto!" She pulled back her hood, revealing wide eyes and a grin. The executioner raised his ax. "Mantel says to call to him now. Gorda Fritz has sent the signal. Jeremy Chikalto has entered the Haze."

***

Jeremy swam with Maren and Lyrna to the edge of the tunnel towards the purple beyond. His body pushed against some gravity that kept him centered in the tunnel. But Maren and Lyrna's bodies resisted the boundaries of the tunnel, as if they were fish too large to slip through the holes of a net, and the current sucked them fiercely towards the bright light. Jeremy yanked with all his might and they finally popped through the membrane to the other side. Jeremy held tight to his unconscious charges and kept swimming.

"Jeremy... Mantel, letum libero everto!" said another voice.

The further they floated from the tunnel, the thicker the purple Haze became. A flash of red light brought Jeremy to a halt. A scream punctured the Haze and a bloody corpse appeared before him, accompanied by two huge black bears who snarled at him. Jeremy startled and thrashed away from this ghastly trio, tightening his grip on Maren and Lyrna. He looked back at the tunnel—*maybe it was a mistake to leave it*—and saw more animals and corpses scattered around the Haze.

"Why are there..." Jeremy shielded his brow and squinted. The Haze seemed to go on indefinitely and every now and then a new creature materialized, as though it had popped out of a fold in space.

"Jeremy Chikalto! Come. Mantel is here!" Now it was a man's voice to his right. It sounded desperate.

He had to focus. He had to follow the voices. Jeremy touched Maren's wrist and felt a slow pulse. Lyrna's nose twitched. *Just asleep*, Jeremy reassured himself, but he wasn't entirely convinced.

"Jeremy." Jeremy swam towards the voice. Who was Mantel? Why did the voice keep changing? They were all coming from the same direction.

In the distance a mass of something appeared and floated towards them. As it drew closer, Jeremy saw a crowd of massacred bodies shrouded in a pink mist. A fizdruft, like Lyrna in stature but with a black and orange coat, glided through the air, pulling a thread attached to the body of a middle-aged man. The man was rocking back and forth, repeating, "Samantha, I'm sorry Samantha!" Blood spilled from a bullet wound in his head. The fizdruft and man disappeared behind a dark purple cloud.

Now shades of gray swirled past him. The tunnel that Jeremy had originally entered was out of sight. He was close to the source of the voices. "Jeremy. Almost..."

Through the purple clouds, Jeremy could see the young woman who now spoke his name. Her head was almost completely severed from her body, hanging by a mere flap of skin. She pointed to a jagged rip in the fabric of Haze where she had recently entered. Around the rip swirled opposing forces of white and black. "Exit there! Hurry!" she yelled in one breath. Then an animal Jeremy had never seen before, a tiger-like creature with huge fangs, grabbed hold of a thread that extended from the woman's sternum, and pulled her past him. Even with her head nearly severed, a wide smile spread across her face, her pupils enlarged and menacing. "For Mantel!" she whispered before disappearing out of sight.

Jeremy floated towards the rip, which seemed to be attracting and repelling him simultaneously, and pushed Lyrna through to the other side. He held Maren in his other arm. Jeremy turned around for one final contemplation of the Haze, and saw an elk racing towards him. At the last second, the elk pivoted and Jeremy saw it was towing a disemboweled man. "Help me, please!" the man cried, and as he passed, he grabbed Maren by the arm. The elk galloped away, dragging the man by the chord connected to his sternum, and Maren was ripped from Jeremy's arms. The man, the elk, and Maren disappeared into inky purple rays. "Maren!" he cried, and he rushed after her, but he couldn't match the galloping elk. *Maren, I'm sorry!* As Jeremy swam desperately, the purple turned to a shade of crimson, collapsing in on itself.

Then, a bright pinpoint flashed onto the crimson and zigzagged into the air, tearing open with a sound like a rusty zipper. The fissure burned molten red. Scaly arms shoved through the gap, followed by a horned head. The eyes turned to Jeremy, and he froze, as they bore hundreds of black bubbles, the multifaceted eyes of a fly. The rest of the creature then birthed its scaly body out of the rift.

In an instant, a boar emerged from a cloud, charging at the scaly creature. The boar's tusks butted the creature's horns and grappled with it, pushing it away from Jeremy. Then the creature burst into flames, gibbering and mewling in pain, and disintegrated into ashes. The boar grunted and then trotted away.

Jeremy blinked. *What..?! Maren's gone!* Jeremy looked around the Haze, his pulse quickening, his breath now erratic. In the distance, he could see the outline of a lion. It was bounding towards him, snarling. Jeremy kicked backwards towards the rip where Lyrna had exited, and climbed into it. His whole body churned and buzzed and he warped out of the Haze and onto a patch of grass. He was out of the wine-dark sea and back on terra firma. His body rattled with each breath and tingled from head to toe. He rolled over, coughing. Lyrna lay curled up at his side in an uneasy sleep. Blood covered the grass and pooled nearby on a large, flat stone tablet. Drag marks led into the trees.

Chapter 11

Kidnapped

Gillian and Mateo sat in the docking bay pavilion, waiting for Maren, Jeremy, and Lyrna to return. The eclipse had ended and rays of light streamed down through knobby trees. The wind had settled into a light breeze. Gillian let down her blonde hair and clipped her barrette to the side of her dress.

"Do you think Maren likes Jeremy?"

"I doubt it, she's too sensible." Mateo patted his belly. "I hope they bring leftovers."

"And I do absolutely adore Raaychila and Wantoro, it's a shame Jeremy isn't more like them."

"He's like his mother," said Mateo.

"He most certainly is not!"

"The dancing, the singing, both are a bit wacky, you've said so yourself."

"Raaychila is sweet, that makes a world of a difference."

Mateo laughed and stood up, stretching his arms overhead. "Hey look, I think that's them." He frowned. Gillian stood beside her husband and squinted, shading her brow with her hand.

The IIU and Ms. Fritz emerged from the forest path just beyond the stretch of pavilions. They walked briskly to the Nononia's spaceship.

Gillian and Mateo ran forward. Bentley raised his hand.

"Please, stay where you are," said Bentley. The other IIU members stood beside him while Ms. Fritz shuffled behind.

"What's happened? Where's Maren and Jeremy?" Gillian's eyes darted back and forth. Mateo remained silent.

Bentley brought his hand down. "Gillian, Mateo, I'm afraid someone has kidnapped your daughter and the Cajjez. We've called in a full IIU search team and they'll be arriving shortly. All space travel patrols have been notified. Please remain in your craft until further notification."

CHAPTER 12

THE LONG LOST SON

Jeremy parted a swarm of flies with his hand. He nudged Lyrna, who lay unconscious next to him, her chest rising and falling with each tiny breath. "Lyrna! Lyrna, wake up!" But the fizdruft wouldn't rouse.

The grass around Jeremy was streaked and splotched with blood, and a gory stone slab stood at the center of the glade. The area was enclosed by evergreens, and on one side, craggy rocks rose into the sky. Jeremy breathed deeply and listened to birds chattering in the pines, until the moment was cracked by a gun shot.

Lyrna opened her eyes wide and leapt to her feet. She puffed, hissed, jerked her head from left and right, and finally dashed into some shrubs.

Jeremy stood up, his heart pounding. "Maren's gone, Lyrna. Maren's gone." He stared at the gory stone slab, and his stomach turned. "Whoever did this must have run off when they heard gunshots. Unless...?" Jeremy pointed to the drag marks leading from the stone slab to the woods. "I don't like this. We have to get out of here." Jeremy crept to the shrubs. "Come on, Lyrna! Let's go!"

"Lyrna bad dream!"

It felt that way, but no. Jeremy saw the Haze and the faces of the dead, still wriggling in that space in between. The Haze. What was it? "It wasn't a dream. We went behind the air. We have to go now."

Lyrna poked her head out of the leaves, parting them with her whiskers. "Blood ground. Where Maren? Fritz?"

Jeremy backed away and ran in the direction opposite the drag marks. He couldn't think of her now. He'd lost Maren. What did that mean, to lose someone in that place? The thought forced its way to the surface: he'd killed her. "Come on," he managed, fighting back tears. Lyrna scurried after him.

The air was warm and the sun was high in the sky. Birds circled overhead, squawking. Jeremy peered up at the tree tops, the foliage thicker and greener than anything he'd ever seen before.

"Where?" asked Lyrna.

"I don't know. We're not on Findle anymore."

"Lyrna hate black orb."

Jeremy and Lyrna trekked through the woods until they came across a stained mattress propped up against a thick tree stump. The ground was littered with beer cans.

Jeremy sat against the stump. He picked up a beer can and analyzed the label. "Busch Light, never heard of it. Where do you think we are?" Lyrna jumped onto the splotched mattress, and began licking her paw. Jeremy dropped the beer can and snatched Lyrna by the ear tuft, pulling her off the mattress. "Don't go on that! That's disgusting."

Lyrna grunted and settled beside him on the grass, watching the crows as they circled and swooped. The Cajjez buried his head in his hands, raking his hair with his fingertips. Where did that creature take Maren? Had he made a mistake following the voices? The being he saw in the Haze, the one with the severed head—she was not an angel, she was a dead woman. And there was the scaly thing. He shuddered. "I just don't understand, Lyrna."

"Maren come soon," said Lyrna hopefully.

"No, I don't think so."

Then a gunshot scattered the crows, who squawked and flapped away. Jeremy and Lyrna jumped. The gun was close. A large, sandy-colored dog ran past, splattering drool across Jeremy's cheek. Jeremy wiped it with his sleeve in disgust, leaving a streak of blood, dirt, and spit.

"Well, now looky here!" A big, ruddy face pocked with acne appeared inches away from Jeremy's own. Jeremy gasped and pressed his back against the stump.

A man wearing green camouflage bent over and put his hands on his knees. "And a kitty cat, too!"

"Are we on Findle?" asked Jeremy.

The man adjusted the shoulder strap holding his shotgun. "Findle! What do you mean Findle, boy? Let's get 'er up." The man gripped Jeremy's forearm and lifted him to his feet. Examining him, "How old are you, young man? Too young to be drinkin', I see that much. Tell me straight: are you boozin' out here?" The man slapped Jeremy on the back with his leathery hand and let out a guffaw. Jeremy stumbled forward.

"No, no I'm not... but, well have you seen a girl? She has blonde hair and gray eyes. She's about my height?"

"Nope."

"Stinky man beast!" mewed Lyrna.

"What'd you say, boy?" The man straightened his back and stared down at Jeremy.

"A girl–"

"No, after that!"

Jeremy grimaced and turned his head. The man's breath was a mix of onions, cigarettes and whiskey. "I didn't say anything."

"What? You didn't say nothin'? I heard you!"

"Lyrna said your breath stinks." Jeremy shrugged. "We're not on Findle? Where are we?"

The man spat on the ground and then looked at Lyrna. She hissed and hid behind Jeremy's leg. "Funny," said the man. "You're real funny. You got a talkin' cat, huh?"

"She's a fizdruft."

"Mmhm, let's take you back to my place and get you warshed up, and you can tell me all 'bout your fuzzrat and that blood you got on your face. Then we'll get you back to your folks. I seen your buddies here the other week, drinking, carryin' on, and they set my trash can on fire, nearly set the woods aflame too. I've half a mind to call the cops, but no, I'm handlin' this civil like." The man knelt to the ground and grabbed an unopened beer can. Popping the tab, he guzzled it down and then tossed the can onto the mattress. "Name's Bill, by the way. Hey! Chester!" Bill whistled and hollered and soon the large canine bounded back to its owner. "Don't go boozin' by my house again. All right? This way."

Chester gave Lyrna two disinterested sniffs before leading the party back to Bill's house.

It was a fifteen-minute walk. A trail led the way through tall pine trees and across makeshift bridges over streams swollen with recent rain. The place was humid. Beads of dew clung to a spider web. Jeremy counted twenty webs on his way to Bill's house to keep his mind busy. Ms. Fritz wanted him to come here. This is where the voices in the Haze led him, so he'd see it through, then make his way home. Bill's house was a cottage that boasted a porch with a water-worn picnic table and a wood-burning stove. The cottage was painted a pale blue, which was chipped in places.

"You *live* here?" asked Jeremy. He'd only ever read descriptions of squalor, which in his summation, was the only word to describe such a residence.

"And I'll probably die here. My great grandpa built this place with his own two hands. Family-owned mountain lot, yep." The man belched and called out to his wife. "Henrietta! Hey Hen! Come on out and take a look at what I've scrounged up!" Bill winked at Jeremy and whistled a folksy melody. The door creaked open and out poked the head of a young man who looked a couple of years older than Jeremy.

"Who's that?" said the young man.

"Forgot to ask, would you believe it, Jason! Go get your Ma. Your Ma will set things right."

Before Jeremy could offer his name, the son's head disappeared back into the house. The son shouted, "Hey, Ma! Pa's brought a guy home!" and within a few seconds, the son reemerged, followed by his mother. Henrietta was a round, solid woman. Her cheeks were flushed apples and her thin gray hair clung to her forehead. She was sweaty from cooking. Spaghetti sauce splattered her white apron decorated with kittens.

"Hello there! What a fine, handsome young man!" began Henrietta. She looked Jeremy up and down, her smile broadening with each passing second. "Handsome, indeed!"

Bill laughed. "Don't expect much out of him, we walked 'bout a mile and he ain't said a peep. In his own world, this one."

Jason pushed past his father and stood directly in front of the Cajjez, putting his lanky arms on his hips. "Probably 'cause you didn't ask him his name! Hey, so what's your name?"

Jeremy straightened up, but he wasn't quite as tall as Jason. "Cajjez Jeremy Chikalto."

Jason squinted and batted a fly away from his brow. "Cajjez what? Jeremy?"

"Cajjez is my title. I'm sorry, you don't recognize me? Where am I?"

Henrietta stepped forward and untied her apron. "So, what brings you around these parts? Bill, what's the story?" She kept her eyes on Jeremy. Despite being covered in mud and blood, he was such a delightful sight, it was hard to look away.

"Found him 'bout a mile or so away in the woods. Got blood on his face and he had beer cans all 'round him. I'm thinking he's one of those teens we got troubling us, but we'll make it right."

"Is he lost? Jeremy, what were you doing out in those woods by yourself?" There was concern in her voice. "Why're you bleeding?"

Jeremy shielded his eyes from the sunlight. He'd have to think on his feet. "I don't know. I think I hit my head."

"Where you from?"

"Watico." Jeremy pet Chester, the golden retriever, who had begun to lick his hand.

"Where on Earth is Watico?"

"What?" Jeremy started laughing, but the laugh was all wrong. It was a deep, shaky laugh and when he felt it start to change into a cry, he swallowed it down. "As in, 'Where on Earth is Professor von Hest?'" Why were they referencing a childrens' game?

"What on Earth are you talking about? Oh dear," said Henrietta. "And where are your parents?"

Jeremy felt a lump form in the back of his throat. "They're far, far away, I guess. Why do you keep saying Earth?"

"Earth is our home, child. It's home to all God's creatures. And he's sent you to us. Bill, we'd better get him inside and cleaned up for supper. We'll sort this out, figure out his folks." Henrietta disappeared back inside the cottage.

Jeremy's head spun. Earth? How did he get on Earth? Had Ms. Fritz sent him to Earth, and how did she know going behind the air would get him here? Jeremy's hands started to tremble, but he had to get through this. He had to orient himself. A strange, heavy feeling traveled down his head, through his limbs. It was a detached sensation and he felt his brain numb over, as though an icy fog had left him sluggish and forgetful. He'd float through this, it was the only way forward.

By the time Jeremy cleaned himself with a warm, wet dish rag, the Truist family was struck by his celebrity-like appearance and manners. Electricity seemed to spark all around him. Lyrna too began to take on an extraordinary quality. She looked more like a wild desert cat than any house cat the Truist family had ever seen. Lyrna's gray ears with black tufts had the most peculiar habit of twitching whenever anyone looked her way.

Dinner was pasta with spaghetti sauce. Henrietta pressured Jeremy into drinking goat's milk, a sight that delighted the entire family. Jeremy spit it all over the floor, and Henrietta fussed over the mess. Dessert was donuts. Jeremy was familiar with donuts, and ate a plain one in silence, but it only made his stomach hurt.

"So where is Watico?" continued Henrietta between gulps of goat's milk.

Her son Jason glared. "Never heard of Watico. Place sounds made up and ridiculous."

Jeremy tried to rouse himself to answer, but found it difficult to speak through the fog. He could play dumb, really lean into the idea that he was hurt. At least the Earth Scholars' observation missions on Earth hadn't been compromised. Earth really was isolated. "I don't know. I can't remember much. Gosh, I wish I could remember how I hit my head," he lied.

"But Ma, I saw when he was cleanin' himself that he wasn't bleedin' from the head. He only got it on his hands and a streak across his face." Jason's brows knitted together.

"Shush! The boy's got the amnesia." Henrietta stood up from her seat and began clearing the plates away.

Bill leaned forward on his elbows, his eyes following his wife. "You know, I thought he was actin' funny! He told me his cat was sayin' somethin' 'bout me, and I thought, boy, maybe he had a drink too many. Place was littered with beer cans!"

Henrietta shook her head. "No, no. This young man ain't drunk. I'd a known if he were, have enough experience with you. That's the devil in those drinks. We ain't wantin' any more of the devil's influence in this house. I'd recognize a drunk. He's serious and don't remember how he hit his head. He's confused and distressed, clear as day." Henrietta scrubbed the plates with extra vigor before setting them in the dish rack.

Jeremy pet Lyrna, who had settled on his lap. She looked up at him and was about to speak. Jeremy interrupted. "No! No, Lyrna."

"What is it?" said Henrietta, looking up from the dishes.

"Lyrna scratched me was all."

Lyrna hissed.

Jason eyed Jeremy and Lyrna from across the table. "That's a big cat you got there, a strange lookin' cat. It's an exotic animal, like a lynx or something." Jason smiled and crossed his arms. "Worth a lot. How'd you get it?"

Jeremy ignored him. "So," continued Jeremy, "where am I exactly?"

"Endless Mountains of Pennsylvania." This time it was Bill who spoke, though he continued to look down at the comics section of the newspaper.

"And now where did you say your parents were?" Henrietta abandoned the pile of dishes in the sink and stood beside Jeremy. She placed a hand on his shoulder.

"I..." Jeremy looked at his lap. "What I mean is, I don't have any parents." Jeremy's eyes glazed over with tears. He couldn't think of them. *I'm not. I'm not. It's a lie. My parents are well.* What were his parents doing now? Had they discovered he was missing? They would be absolutely gutted. Why did he ever agree to leave home?

"Oh heavens! No parents! Do you remember your parents? Bill, did you hear this? Bill!" Henrietta marched over to Bill and tore the newspaper out from his hands.

Another wave of detachment washed over Jeremy. He had to survive now. He needed his wits about him. "No. I don't remember much of anything, except for I know I'm an orphan."

This time, Lyrna did scratch Jeremy. Jeremy winced in pain.

Henrietta gripped the table and began rocking back and forth.

Bill stiffened in his seat. "Oh no, Henrietta!" said Bill.

Henrietta's rocking only intensified. "Oh Lord, oh Lord. I've got a feelin', Bill. I've got a feelin'."

"Henrietta, let's go you and me talk 'bout this out back."

"I've got a feelin', Bill. Oh Lord. Oh Lord. Do you not recognize the Lord's infinite mercy?" At this, Henrietta burst into tears. Bill escorted her out of the kitchen, leaving Jeremy and Lyrna perplexed. Jason averted his eyes from them and leaned in for another helping of donuts. Jeremy pet Lyrna. After making eye contact with his fizdruft, he mouthed, "Please don't talk."

Jason frowned and shook his head. "Jeremy, you've gone and pulled at my parents' heartstrings just as they were starting to heal. My family don't need this rollercoaster." He got up and left the table.

That night, Jeremy was put up in Jason's bedroom, a small room with low ceilings and faded yellow wallpaper. A tree outside scratched against the side of the house. Jason, who was used to the menacing sound, slept soundly on the hardwood floor. Jeremy was given Jason's bed, which was well-worn and mostly clean thanks to Henrietta's clean, starched sheets. Jeremy shivered. He did not want to stay at the Truist's for long, but needed to gather as much information about Pennsylvania as possible. He knew enough about Earth to get by—some different countries, continents, religions. But he didn't recall Pennsylvania.

Should I ask about Mantel? Ms. Fritz had told him to seek out Mantel. But then... Ms. Fritz had almost killed Maren. And the Intergalactic Intelligence Unit—what to make of them? And Maren! Would he ever see her again? Jeremy's head pounded the more he thought about his day, the purple Haze, and his separation from Maren. Nothing made sense. *This is all on me*, Jeremy thought, *I'm supposed to do something*. Jeremy waited for a sign that night, watching the air for some hint of movement, and nothing happened.

But then, something did happen. It was nearing three in the morning and the wind howled outside. Jeremy had only just closed his eyes when a creak outside the bedroom door awoke him. He gripped the pillow he had been using—an off-white, flimsy thing with several mysterious stains and the smell of pine soap—and turned towards the door. His pulse quickened as the door knob opened. And then it all happened so fast: Jeremy was seized in the dark and smothered, as an intense force gripped his body. There was shaking, sobbing, and finally, a release. Jeremy blinked.

"Jeffrey! It's my Jeffrey come home!" Henrietta's face flickered in candlelight, her cheeks red and swollen. Bill stood in the doorway behind her holding a candle, his face skeptical.

"What?" said Jeremy.

Jason sat up on the floor and rubbed his eyes, "What're you sayin'? Ma, it's the middle of the night!"

"Don't you see? It's your brother Jeffrey come home at last! This boy is your brother Jeffrey!"

"Jeffrey, can't be–impossible," said Jason. He turned to Jeremy and then back to his mom. "Jeffrey isn't coming home. Mom, please! Don't do this to yourself!"

Jeremy looked around him. The wind continued to howl outside the house. He pushed the pillow away from his head and stood up, irritated. "I'm sorry, I'm not Jeffrey. I am *Jeremy*. But I feel like there's a lot of emotion in the room, and I—I," Jeremy stood up and moved towards the door. "Thank you for the hospitality and I'm sorry to bother you, but I should get going. Come on Lyrna."

Lyrna stood up, stretched, and readied herself at Jeremy's heels.

"You aren't going nowhere, Jeffrey." Henrietta steadied herself in the door frame and thrust out her arms. Outside the window the clouds cleared and moonlight cast a bluish tint over her skin. "The Lord spoke to me tonight, and he said, 'Henrietta, this is your charge. You were a bad, faithless mother once. Redeem yourself. See that you don't lose him again.' You were so scared, Momma's little baby. 'Henrietta!' he said, 'The Lord works in mysterious ways!' and I heard him! And I know, Jeffrey, that things are gonna be all right now!" Henrietta pursed her face, still swollen from tears. Her breathing was erratic.

Jeremy shivered. *Maybe some entity had spoken with her? I was given a message, Ms. Fritz had some otherworldly encounter. And then I was in the Haze. Anything's possible.* He bit his fingernails and surveyed the room's inhabitants. How to proceed? Who's Jeffrey? At last, he said, "You received a message? I have too. To come here…"

Henrietta's eyes shone. "Lord! Thank you, Lord!" She rushed forward to hug Jeremy once more.

Bill and Jason's mouths were agape. They began to rejoice and rushed forward to hug some piece of Jeremy not contained entirely within Henrietta's grasp.

Lyrna, alarmed and puffed, sidestepped the emotional faux-reunion, unsure of whether to attack or wait for it to end. "Lyrna say bad, bad."

CHAPTER 13

MAREN AWAKES

Maren awoke in the back of an ambulance. She blinked. Had she died? A mask covered her nose and mouth, and her eyes widened. She struggled and pulled on her restraints. "Where am I? What's happening?!" Her voice was muffled.

"Relax. You need more oxygen, just keep breathing," said a paramedic, securing the mask to her face. The driver called from the front of the vehicle.

"How's she doing back there?"

"Her skin's got some color back."

"Great news. Hey, got a call to bypass the front of the NYU Medical Center, so we'll have to take her through the back."

Maren mumbled through the oxygen mask and twisted her head. The ambulance worker lifted the mask. "Yeah?"

"Where am I?" she repeated between breaths.

"New York."

"New York? Where's New York? *That* New York?!"

The paramedic lowered the mask over her face. "Hey Sam, she's not doing as good as I thought."

CHAPTER 14

THE CALL

Jeremy's mother played the piano on a platform in the corner of the room. Light streamed through velvet curtains and shone on Raaychilla's lustrous hair, which cascaded down her black dress. Wantoro, seated in an armchair, tapped his fingers and noted how each song his wife played grew increasingly vehement.

A messenger entered the chambers with news that the Nononias had been reached. Wantoro nodded and waited for Raaychila to conclude her song.

The walk to the Communications Center was silent. Raaychila was nervous about Jeremy. Wantoro was nervous about Jeremy's reputation. Only a week had passed since Jeremy departed for Lejjone Panil, and already they were receiving a call from his caretakers. Wantoro and Raaychila had been arguing about Jeremy and missed the call, but it was classified as urgent.

Six guards stood at the entrance to the Communications Center, a vast control room which monitored flight traffic, weather, and planet conditions. Offices, divided by white screens, lined the back walls. Wantoro and Raaychila were led to one of these offices and seated in front of a large monitor. The Communications Director initiated video conferencing.

Three individuals appeared on the screen, each wearing a white jumpsuit with a red flame etched on the breast. Raaychila tensed.

"Intergalactic Intelligence Unit, Special Force 64, reporting," said Bentley, his thick brow casting a shadow over his face. He bowed.

Wantoro frowned and he reached for Raaychila's hand. He had expected to talk directly to the Nononias. "We received a call earlier from the Nononias and I understand you have information for us concerning Cajjez Jeremy."

"We do sir," said Bentley. "He and Maren Nononia have been kidnapped."

CHAPTER 15

OUT THE WINDOW

Back in Pennsylvania, Jeremy spent the next few days trying to stomach the affections of Henrietta Truist. He was able to piece together that she had irresponsibly left her three-year-old son Jeffrey in a pasture on the south side of the mountain, about a mile away from the Truist residence, in order to prepare dinner. "You were always makin' a fuss back then, hollerin' and pullin' your hair out," she had said. Jeffrey's older brother, Jason, was five at the time and was helping Bill build a tree stand for hunting deer. When Henrietta returned to the pasture on the south side of the mountain to retrieve Jeffrey, he was nowhere to be found. Police were contacted and neighbors helped with the search, but the boy was never recovered. Henrietta had prayed daily for the return of her son. She had taken solace in her religion, which was both familiar in its teachings and strange to Jeremy. It seemed a version of Christianity, but one with talismans and rituals, and a heavy emphasis on evil spirits.

"Here—you read this now," she shoved a pamphlet into Jeremy's lap as he sat cross-legged on Jason's floor. "We'll have devotions tonight and I want you familiar with our healin' script. We'll get you looked at by our Deliverance Minister soon, don't you worry, baby."

"I'll take a look," said Jeremy. He patted the pamphlet and waited for her to leave.

"Okay, and Jason will be back from school soon, so try to get right on that so he don't distract you."

Jeremy nodded and she left. Then he cast the pamphlet aside. It felt wrong to pretend to be her lost son. It was gnawing at Jeremy's conscience, but he felt like he had to stick around long enough for his purpose to be made clear. *This couldn't all just be coincidence.* His heart panged for his own mother and father, and he recognized the Truists' longing for the son they lost.

Jeremy heard some chatter coming from outside and peered out the window. Jason had brought a friend home with him and they were trekking up the path to the house.

Jeremy cracked the window open and listened.

"Adam," said Jason. "You'll see. He's a weirdo. Probably laying on the floor, staring up at the ceiling. Seen him doing this meditation thing the other day. Oh, hey Ma."

Henrietta had bustled outside. "Dang it, Jason! Dang it! I'll have to make more soup. Hello Adam, nice to see you." Henrietta swooped in on Adam, planting a slobbery kiss on his cheek.

Adam smiled and shied away from Henrietta. He pushed shaggy hair off his face. "Hello, Mrs. Truist. Jason's been telling me so much about Jeffrey, can't wait to see him. My folks wanna come down and see him this weekend, too, if that's all right."

"Of course! My Jeffrey's a real light, a beacon. Tell your parents they can come along back to our place after Church on Sunday for the Deliverance. I'll fix us a nice brunch."

"Sure thing, Mrs. Truist."

Henrietta led the way into the house and Jason and Adam followed. The smell of boiling vegetables permeated the house. "Jeffrey!" hollered Henrietta. Nothing. "Jason, why don't you go and fetch your brother, he's probably hidin' in your room with that cat of his."

Jason and Adam entered Jason's bedroom and found Jeremy laying on the center of the floor, staring up at the ceiling.

"Told ya," snickered Jason, digging his elbow into Adam's side. "What're you doin'?"

Adam stifled a laugh, amused at the contrast between the two supposed brothers.

Jeremy took his time responding. "Hey. Deep in thought here. Care to join me?"

"What are you looking at? Got a spider up there or something?" Jason looked to Adam and shook his head.

So Jason had seen him meditating earlier. And so what? What did it matter? He needed to get out of this place. "If I concentrate on a spot above your bed, the air bleeds purple. Right up there." Jeremy pointed, and then dexterously jumped to his feet. "I'm hungry." He spun himself out the door, then leapt down the entire flight of stairs, landing with a thud at the bottom, then clapped for himself.

Jason turned to Adam. "See what I mean? He's just weird. Ain't all there. He's not my brother."

Adam flinched.

"Don't worry 'bout him hearing us," continued Jason. "He talks right past me all the time. He knows I got no idea what he's talkin' about and still he goes on. I want him gone."

Henrietta dragged an extra chair inside the kitchen from the outside deck to make room for Adam. She rang the dinner bell and within seconds, Bill, Jason, and Adam assembled around the table. They looked at the staircase and Lyrna hopped down, followed by Jeremy, who descended the steps slowly.

"Ma, he brought his cat again to supper!" said Jason, jabbing a finger in the air towards Lyrna as Jeremy entered the room. Lyrna produced a deep-throated growl.

"Lyrna stays," said Jeremy as he pulled out his seat at the head of the table.

"Ma," continued Jason, "it can't keep going on like this."

Bill interrupted, "It's all right, Jason." He glanced at Henrietta. "Jeffrey's still gettin' settled in is all."

Adam took a seat beside Jeremy. "So Jeffrey, where'd you go all them years anyway? I helped look for you with my parents way back then, when you first disappeared."

Jeremy placed his hands behind his head and reclined. "I can't tell you." Henrietta spooned a generous helping of soup into Jeremy's bowl.

"Let's begin, shall we?" said Henrietta after she had served the others and seated herself. Everyone held hands and bowed their heads in prayer. Henrietta waited until everyone was still before continuing. "Dear Lord, thank you once again for bringin' my family together and blessing us with the return of Jeffrey. I am insignificant. I am a shell, a shadow-self walking in the valley of death and you give me blood and nourish me. Through faith, you delivered me. Be mindful of our devils and help us put them to rest. We are—"

"Air!" cried Lyrna and she jumped off Jeremy's lap and leapt through the dog flap on the kitchen door. Jeremy stood up.

"Now what?" said Bill, looking towards Jeremy.

Henrietta shrieked, "We do not interrupt prayer–it's blasphemous! Bill! Close your eyes! Jeffrey, be seated."

"But Ma!" said Jason, also rising from the table. "Didn't you hear that cat talk just now?"

"I heard it say 'Air'!" Adam chimed in.

Henrietta remained seated and closed her eyes tightly, wrinkles straining along the corners. She gripped the table, her knuckles turning white. "Boys, we do NOT interrupt prayer. Everyone, sit!"

"But Ma!"

"Jason, devils will fester in you if you give 'em voice!"

"But Ma! It's Jeffrey!"

Henrietta opened her eyes in time to see Jeremy exit through the kitchen door.

CHAPTER 16

LIGHTNING

Lyrna's whiskers twitched as she raced towards the dark presence. A trail behind the house led gently downhill and Lyrna followed it to its base where a small clearing opened up, a scarecrow at its center. Lyrna halted before creeping towards the scarecrow. The scarecrow was moldy and covered in bird droppings, its left arm drooping to the ground, straw spilling out onto the earth. A red smile was stitched across its face, leering at Lyrna. Lyrna tensed and took a step closer. Just beside the scarecrow bubbled a small sulfur pool. Its acrid smell curled Lyrna's whiskers and she sneezed.

"Lyrna!" called Jeremy, just behind the house at the top of the trail.

"Hot pool! Stinky bad, bad!" mewed Lyrna.

Jeremy ran down the trail and saw smoke rising from the hot spring in front of Lyrna. "What is it? Lyrna don't get too close to it." Jeremy caught a whiff of sulfur and turned his face away. "What's going on?"

"Ground open. Bad!"

This was it. This was the sign he'd been waiting for. "Was it one of those earthquakes Ms. Fritz had been studying? Did the ground shake? I didn't feel anything!" Jeremy knelt in front of the hot spring and examined the bubbling water, shielding his nose with his shirt sleeve. "Did the air twitch?"

"No. Air bad," said Lyrna.

"What do you mean? You think it's a sign, right?"

Lyrna hissed. "Bad!" She hopped from paw to paw.

Jeremy ran his hands through his hair and then leaned in closer to the hot spring. A bubble on the surface of the pool burst and sprayed a few drops of hot liquid onto his face. Jeremy winced and pulled back.

"No good, bad!" Lyrna hissed.

Jeremy stood up and leaned over the hot spring, the sway of a heated breeze steaming his face, a tempting dance that whispered the secrets of the Earth, ancient and elemental. "Lyrna," he whispered. "It's breathtaking."

"Jeffrey, step away from that devil's sulfur!" said Henrietta from atop the hill. Behind her, Bill cradled a rifle. Jason and his friend Adam stood stupefied in the shadows. "Boy, I said back away from that spot!"

"Evil!" said Lyrna, now puffed as she circled around the hot spring.

"Lord Almighty, Bill," said Henrietta, turning to her husband. "It really is talking. Shoot it."

Bill raised his rifle and aimed it at Lyrna. His finger squeezed the trigger.

A shot rang out, and the muzzle of Bill's rifle flashed yellow in the dusk. At the same time, a blue streak of light zapped in front of Jeremy and Lyrna. The bullet fell to the ground and bounced. The blue light then retracted back into Jeremy's hands. For a few breathless moments, Jeremy stood before the Truist family in shock, his hair frizzy with static. Then Jeremy collapsed to the ground.

Chapter 17

The Trail

Henrietta crossed herself as she walked down the trail behind the house towards Jeremy and Lyrna. She groped a tree and fixed her eyes on Jeremy, who was motionless and sprawled on his stomach. "Lord, protect me from evil," she mumbled, at last reaching him and placing her hands on the small of his back.

Bill watched in horror and then nudged Jason. "Go on, get some help from the Watsons. Go down next door, round up some folks from the church and tell 'em what you saw. Take the truck." Jason grabbed Adam by the shoulder and the two sprinted to the front yard.

Jeremy came to and felt weak. He opened his eyes and saw Henrietta standing above him. His mind swarmed. *Did Bill just try to shoot Lyrna? Did I just zap?* Jeremy craned his neck towards Lyrna, who crouched low and moved towards him. She licked Jeremy's hand. "You have to hide," said Jeremy.

106

"Jeremy, I mean no harm to you or your fuzzrat. It was a mistake," said Henrietta, standing straighter. Her eyes were wild and her lips trembled as she spoke. She crossed herself and looked at Lyrna. "That's a nice kitty. Sshh, there now."

Lyrna hissed.

"Did you summon this devil's pool?" She gestured to the hot spring. The wind picked up and the arm of the scarecrow collapsed to the ground. Henrietta flinched and looked back to the top of the hill. Bill had taken a seat in the grass and was staring cautiously ahead. He nodded at her.

"Get me some water," said Jeremy.

"Yes, of course baby." Henrietta looked at the bubbling spring, swallowed, and then shuffled up the hill.

Jeremy spoke to Lyrna as soon as Henrietta was out of earshot. "Did you see that? I had this energy come out of me! I felt it through my hands, and then it went in here." He pointed to his sternum.

"Shoot at Lyrna!" whispered Lyrna, her ears tucked back. "He did. I know. We have to get out of here." Jeremy looked up at the top of the hill and saw that Bill was still sitting there cradling his rifle. However, he was staring intently at the house.

"He's watching Henrietta. They'll try to shoot you again. We can run to those bushes on the count of three."

Lyrna nodded.

"One... two... THREE!" Jeremy sprang for the bushes and Lyrna raced beside him. Seconds later they were enclosed in dark green shrubs. It was easy for Lyrna to maneuver through the underbrush, but Jeremy got scratched and even tripped over an exposed tree root. The woods thinned out as the ground sloped. Jeremy and Lyrna continued down the hill. They stopped at a trail that crossed in front of them.

"What do you think, Lyrna?" Jeremy tried to steady his breath.

Lyrna looked left and then right, but only mewed in response.

"This way then!" Jeremy took a deep breath before turning right and running as fast as he could.

CHAPTER 18

DESTINATION EARTH

Ms. Fritz sat at a sleek black table in the IIU Mothership, which was docked at a secret outpost just outside Watico's jurisdiction. The red and black décor glowed as she flicked on her lighter. A cinnamon scented candle soon burned in front of her and she placed her black orb beside it. On the other side of the candle sat a tea saucer and a small plate with a croissant. Ms. Fritz nibbled idly on the croissant and sighed.

She just received word that Wantoro put out a warrant for her arrest, and she was wanted for questioning back on Watico. Ever since Jeremy, Maren, and Lyrna crossed over to the Haze, Ms. Fritz feared that any delay might be disastrous. She needed to get to Earth to meet with Mantel as soon as possible. "So obviously I cannot meet with the Chikalto family."

Bentley nodded. He, along with the other two members of IIU 64, sat across from Ms. Fritz. "We'll have nothing to do with that family now that we've separated Jeremy. We should be receiving the other ships at our space dock shortly."

Ms. Fritz spun around in her chair with a twinkle in her eye. "A four-year journey to Earth! A marriage between scientific achievement and the will of the heavens. Our destiny is achieved in a blink. How I wish I could see the Royal Guards' smug faces once they realize we've plucked their best and brightest from right under their noses. But Bentley,"

"Yes ma'am."

"That's what you get when you fill the most coveted scientific positions with political appointees and yes-men."

"Yes ma'am."

Ms. Fritz lifted her finger, hesitated, then said, "Ready the ship."

Drew held his pale hand to his chest. "Our supplies have been secured aboard the ship."

Ms. Fritz paused and dunked her croissant into her tea, a gesture meant to be dramatic but executed too sloppily. Tea spilled onto her slacks. Ms. Fritz cleared her throat and dabbed at the spill. The IIU pretended not to notice.

"Are you three ready to meet Mantel?" Ms. Fritz was the only one of the party who had actually met Mantel. She was nineteen years old then, and her parents' research into Earth's volcanism had led to that fateful meeting. Gorda

Fritz and her parents were given instructions and sent back to space with the black orb and a prophecy.

Jasmine took a deep breath, "I am ready and willing to serve Mantel in every capacity and understand the fate of us all rides on the passion of my oath."

"Because even though it only takes five years to get to Earth, you know it's a twenty-year return journey. Quite a commitment, Jasmine."

"Only for Mantel."

"Only for Mantel," repeated Bentley and Drew.

Chapter 19

Ensnared

Jeremy and Lyrna sprinted down the trail. Duck a tree limb, jump over a root, turn a corner, repeat. Soon excitement replaced Jeremy's fears. Had he really made a bolt of lightning? Did it have something to do with the Haze? *Something celestial better visit me soon and tell me what to do!* A tree limb snagged Jeremy's shirt, tearing the cotton at the shoulder, and he fell flat on his face.

Lyrna skid in the dirt and backtracked to the Cajjez. "Jeremy! Okay?"

Jeremy lifted his head from the forest floor. His lip was bleeding. He felt around in his mouth. His perfect, white teeth were still in place. Jeremy smiled, spit up dirt and sighed, "Just a busted lip."

"Shoulder cut," said Lyrna.

Jeremy brushed the grass and dirt away from a jagged gash on his shoulder, which was welling up with blood. "Looks deep." Jeremy could feel it now, a dull throbbing down his arm. "It's fine. We have to get out of here." Jeremy got up and they continued to run down the path.

The trail sunk into a marsh studded with gnarled trees. Jeremy paused to take in the new landscape and catch his breath. Then something came flying over the bushes towards Lyrna and him, landing on his face and body, entangling his fingers. They were ensnared in a net. Jeremy thrashed and tried to find the bottom of the netting, but then a large tarp closed over them and blacked out his view. He tumbled to the ground and was then hoisted into the air. Jeremy's heart jumped and Lyrna hissed. They heard voices around them, and the opening of the tarp was shrinking as someone cinched it with rope. Jeremy punched and kicked against the sturdy canvass, but it had little effect. "What are you doing–hey, let us go!"

Lyrna tried to chew through the tarp, but it was pulled so taut, her mouth kept slipping. Between bites, she hissed, "Bad meddlers! Evil spring!"

The men and women outside grew quiet. A man said, "Did you hear that? It's the Devil himself here with us! It said 'evil!'" A woman agreed, "It's true then! Oh poor Henrietta, suffering like this." Another woman chimed in, "But she left her boy, and her punishment needs to play out." "Hasn't she been punished enough?" asked another. And the group started to bicker amongst themselves.

"Excuse me!" Jeremy punched at the tarp. "You don't know who you're dealing with! Let me go! I have a cut on my shoulder. I can't breathe!"

The crowd quieted once more and a man spoke, his voice right next to the other side of the tarp. "We don't bow to no demon." The man spat on the ground, rose, and reinforced the tarp with more rope. "Let's bring 'em back to Henrietta and Bill's then."

Jeremy and Lyrna were tossed onto the flatbed of a truck. The doors slammed and the engine roared. The vehicle lurched forward, jostling the Cajjez and Lyrna over bumpy backroads. Panic began to set in. Jeremy struggled to pry the top of the tarp open, but it only tightened in response. Lyrna continued to slide her mouth along the canvass, trying to catch her teeth on something.

"No shoot Lyrna!" cried Lyrna.

"I won't let them, don't worry." Jeremy massaged his hand, feeling the ghost of power. He slowed his breathing down to the bare minimum, trying not to feel smothered. When they finally arrived at the Truist's, crickets were beginning their night song.

Bill and Henrietta greeted the kidnappers, and Jeremy could hear a dozen other voices among them. Bill slapped someone on the back. "You caught 'em! Oh, thank God. They got away from me and I was about to go after 'em, only was waitin' to hear back from Minister Glibson. Where'd you find 'em?"

"He was almost out to the road, we turn in, see him and the cat lookin' all dazed like a doe and fawn! We tossed our net over 'em, then tied 'em up in Bobby's tarp." The man patted the tarp and laughed.

"Jeffrey," said Henrietta. "Let's get his head out, get him some air now."

The men loosened the tarp and Jeremy's sweat-soaked, bloodied face gasped for breath. He felt too weak to struggle. Everything was happening now as if in a dream.

"We're gonna get you help," said Henrietta.

"Ma, don't get close to him!" said Jason, and he jerked his mother back.

"Okay," said Bill, "we'll haul 'em into the shed in the back. I got more rope and some chains. Jason, get your rabbit cage for the cat."

"Jon, Bob, grab that end of them." Bill and the other men hoisted Jeremy and Lyrna in the tarp and carried them across the yard to the shed. It was an old, rusty shed with a giant metal lock hanging from the open door. The shed had been cleared and the yard nearby was cluttered with old tractor parts, farm tools, and rotted lumber. The men set the tarp down in the corner of the shed. Henrietta followed with a box full of religious paraphernalia.

"Take this, all of you," said Henrietta, shoving deliverance pamphlets, crosses, and rabbits' feet into everyone's hands. "We don't know what they're capable of."

"Can I have some water?" asked Jeremy in a hoarse voice.

"Of course, and now you can't run. I spilled the last cup 'cause you've gone and run off like that. But we'll get you stable, don't you worry Jeffrey." Henrietta left the shed and returned with a glass of water. She poured some into his mouth.

"Lyrna would like some water too."

"Absolutely not."

Lyrna mewed.

Jeremy closed his eyes. "But I need medical attention. My shoulder's cut. Can't you untie me?"

"Nope. Our Minister will decide. You can't be trusted with the devil speakin' through you."

"What are you talking about?" demanded Jeremy.

But Henrietta ignored him and herded everyone out of the shed, closing the door behind her. Jeremy heard the lock click. He closed his eyes and tried to slow his breathing, but couldn't get into a meditative state.

CHAPTER 20

DIVERGENT PATHS

Raaychila fussed with her wardrobe as Wantoro sat motionless in front of the monitor. "What do you think of this?" she asked, tossing a brown knitted overcoat onto the bed. "Or this?" A green, long-sleeved dress landed on top of the overcoat.

"Doesn't matter, sweetheart," said Wantoro.

"Well is it as cold outside as it is inside? You've really blasted the air conditioner."

Wantoro turned from the monitor to examine his wife. Her long, red curls were tangled and her face was tense.

"Well?" she said.

"Raaychila, just wear whatever's comfortable. We're just meeting the IIU at the gates to detain Ms. Fritz for questioning. We'll be outside for a second. And it'll be hours before they even arrive."

Raaychila tossed her head back. "Comfortable! Well, I'm not wearing a brown overcoat as a fashion statement.

Why is it taking hours to bring Fritz here for questioning? Why isn't she here now, why isn't she being questioned now?" Raaychila grabbed the green dress and disappeared into the closet, closing the door behind her.

Wantoro sighed and walked over to the closet door. "They say she has to be processed. And... she asked to speak with a counselor before questioning. That takes time."

"A bunch of bureaucratic nonsense. Our son is missing, Wantoro! Make it happen now, you're the Vor," snapped Raaychila from inside the closet.

"It's the law, dear."

A pause. "And why haven't we heard anything else? What about the search operation? What's being done? Where is the information?"

Wantoro cleared his throat. "Well, we lost communication with the IIU. Apparently, a satellite has malfunctioned."

Raaychila swung the closet door open, and was standing there half-dressed, hands on her hips and eyes blazing. "This is absurd. We have a crisis and suddenly everyone is incompetent?" She slammed the door again.

"I'm sure it will be fixed as soon as possible. Everyone's doing the best they can."

"I'm not waiting for them. I'm going to the IIU Station."

"And why would you do that?"

"Because," said Raaychila, "I'm not waiting around for more mistakes and excuses. I want to talk to Fritz. I want to know what's being done. Someone has to be in charge around here."

"Raaychila!" Wantoro pressed his forehead to the closet door. "You don't have to do that." He tried to sound sweet.

"You can't talk me out of it," Raaychila said after a moment of silence. She emerged from the closet in her green dress and wrapped her arms around Wantoro. "I'll be back in a few hours, love you." Raaychila kissed him and went to her bedside table, grabbing her purse. "If you can't get a hold of me for whatever reason, you can contact Ronny." She left the room.

Raaychila strode down the spaceship landing strip flanked by her six body guards. It was brisk on the roof of the castle, but not as cold as the castle's interior. *Someone really needed to take the air conditioning code away from Wantoro.* She hoped he wasn't too upset, but she would fix that later. Right now, there were more important things.

A V-shaped craft was parked on the landing strip, the engine already purring, and Ronny, the Chief Royal Guard, helped her onto the platform and into the ship. The other body guards followed.

"Vinya Raaychilla, can I get you anything to make you more comfortable?"

"No, that's quite all right Ronny. But thank you." Raaychila took a seat in the cockpit next to Ronny, who flipped some switches, pulled a lever, and radioed the Communications Center for lift off.

Chapter 21

Minister Glibson

Jeremy and Lyrna were still wrapped and tied up in the tarp in the shed. Jeremy's head poked through, and he hoped the fresh air could make its way down to Lyrna. A particularly tight rope was wrapped around the center of the tarp, separating them, but Jeremy managed to push two fingers through and pet Lyrna's head. The shed was dark and cold, and Jeremy took comfort in Lyrna's warm fur.

"So much for our great escape." Jeremy sighed. "Lyrna, whenever the men return, they're going to put you in a cage and I need you to listen to me. Don't talk, don't answer them, and don't hiss if you're angry."

"Lyrna hate place. Hate hot spring."

Jeremy fidgeted. "See, on Earth they don't have fizdrufts so they're scared of you when you talk."

"Hot spring," said Lyrna.

"I know, I know. We'll figure that out later. We have to focus on getting out of here."

Someone coughed outside. The crickets stopped chirping and some voices whispered by the house.

Jeremy took a deep breath and nudged the tarp near Lyrna. "Do you think I'm supposed to go to the hot spring?"

"No!"

"Ssh! Lyrna, please keep your voice down."

"No stinky pool. Death smell."

"I just… I don't know what I'm supposed to do next. You were drawn to it. Seems like it only just appeared. It's got to mean something."

The door to the shed creaked open and a figure entered, a candle lighting up his face. He had wide eyes and furry white eyebrows on a furrowed forehead. Lyrna growled.

"Lyrna, ssh!"

"Jeffrey Truist?" said the man, stepping forward.

"I'm Jeremy Chikalto. I'm sorry. There's been a mistake."

The man motioned for some members of his congregation outside to carry in a wood table. He stroked the table. "There are no mistakes, only lessons. Jeremy, are you a demon?"

"No, I am not a demon!" Jeremy balled his hands into fists. "That's crazy-talk. What's going on?"

"Are you in possession of Jeffrey Truist's body?"

"No, because I'm not Jeffrey Truist. Let me go!"

"Mark 5, verses 2 through 5," the old man scratched his fingernails across the wooden table. "'When Jesus got out of the boat, a man with an evil spirit came from the tombs to meet him.' Jeremy Chikalto, don't you have an evil spirit in you?"

"What? No." The cold seeped in through the damp floorboards. Jeremy pulled his arms to his chest and shivered.

"Jeremy Chikalto, do you swear before God that you do not have supernatural powers?"

"What?" Jeremy rubbed his arms. "What do you mean? If I have a gift, I don't know why."

"Do you have a gift?"

"Maybe I do. Let me go and I'll tell you," said Jeremy through gritted teeth. Lyrna mewed.

"I see, you admit to having an unholy gift. Your family told me that you imitated the lightning of God with your own hands. Can you tell me about this?"

"I-I don't know," Jeremy stammered. "Are you going to help me?"

The old man turned to the congregation crammed in the doorway, each face vying for a glimpse, and nodded. "Now then, Jeremy, this cat of yours—I have reason to believe it's what is known as a witch's familiar."

Lyrna produced a strained mew. Jeremy could tell she was trying her best to suppress a growl.

"No, she's not. She's just my cat."

"A talking cat, saying this is evil, that is evil?"

"No." Jeremy's stomach flipped. He felt sick and exhausted.

"And are you in regular communication with the cat?"

Henrietta pushed through the crowd and waved her arm. "Minister Glibson! I testify that the cat speaks of evil! It says 'evil' then runs and we find a steamin' pool in our yard next to the scarecrow."

Everyone agreed that the cat was unmistakably marked with devilry.

"Silence!" said Minister Glibson, turning back around to the Cajjez. "Do you deny this?"

"Yes, yes, I deny it! Let me out right now! I need to get out of here!"

A murmur swept through the crowd and then Hentrietta slammed her fist on the table. "Minister Glibson, Jeffrey, as I see it and as I've told you both, the Lord blessed me with a second chance. My son returned less than a week ago and I had a feelin' sweep up over me it's my boy come home. I'm startin' to wonder if he's dangerous, always staring off in space and hiding away in rooms by himself with his cat I ain't never liked from the get-go, and then one night at supper it starts talking evil. I heard it, clear as a bell, then it run outside. Jeffrey followed, 'course, and we follow them two and don't you know it, they're conspirin' about evil over a devil's pool! So Jeffrey," Henrietta massaged her crucifix, "we've gone and fetched Minister Glibson and he will get that demon out of you. It's my demon, coming back to haunt me. I'm so sorry." Henrietta burst into tears. Minister Glibson hugged her and then nudged her back into the fold.

"Jeffrey, we will return you," said Minister Glibson, eyes sparkling.

Jeremy thought to try a different approach. It wasn't often that people gathered in awe of such mystic forces, and even if they weren't on the same page, maybe he was meant to share his purpose with them, whatever that was. Jeremy took a deep breath. "Minister Glibson, the truth is I'm not Jeffrey Truist. I'm from the Farmoore Galaxy."

The crowd gasped but were immediately silenced by Minister Glibson with a stern look and a level hand. "Go on, my dear boy."

"A series of events led me here, and it all began with a message from an angel. It said that I had to travel through the Haze and that the end was near. So you might want to... prepare or something. Get your affairs, you know..." Jeremy's pride quickly deflated.

The old man teetered on the edge of the wooden table, his hand trembling. He turned to his flock and said, "Bill, please come here and assist me in releasing the boy from the tarp."

Bill came forward and began to untie the knotted

ropes. Jeremy pushed the tarp down and wriggled out, though he was still constrained by the netting. Bill cut this but then Lyrna burst from her captivity, her claws out and hissing. The crowd recoiled as Lyrna dashed through the congregation and ran off into the night. The women screamed and some of the men ran off after Lyrna, but Minister Glibson remained calm. "Everyone, please settle down. Let's settle down. We'll let the cat go."

Jeremy sighed. Lyrna would be all right. "Could someone help me out?"

Suddenly Minister Glibson shouted, "Grab him!" and all the men fell upon Jeremy and wrestled him down onto the table. Bill looped rope around Jeremy's hands and feet and secured him to the table.

Chapter 22

Besieged

Ronny frowned and tapped on the screen. "Looks like we're getting a signal from the IIU Space Station. We're still out of orbit. Strange to get a request for contact this far out."

"Oh, so now they know how to reach us." Raaychila leaned over the dashboard and pressed the transmit button.

The speaker hissed and then they heard the voice of an air traffic controller. "Your ship is approaching the IIU Space Station. State your name and business and we may grant permission to proceed."

"This is Chief Royal Guard Ronny Bristol, accompanying Vinya Raaychila Chikalto. We'll be docking at the Station in a few minutes and are making an official request for clearance, over."

There was silence on the other end of the transmitter and Raaychila leaned back in her chair. "Can you speed this ship up?"

Static on the other end crackled and a different voice came on the transmitter. "Hello, this is Special Agent Bella Elmav. We're going to have to ask you to redirect to Ongar at this time."

"What? No." Raaychila snapped upright.

The voice continued, "We're doing an emergency repair to an entry dock and all flights are being rerouted to Ongar until further notice."

Ronny furrowed his brow. "I have Vinya Raaychila with me now. We're operating a small, Sub-Class A security vessel, unit 2477 DOX. You're advised to give immediate clearance and we'll use any working entry dock, over."

Raaychila shook her head. "This is ridiculous."

There was more silence on the other end of the transmission.

"Ronny, let's speed up."

Ronny nodded and accelerated. "They know we're coming."

The radio crackled. "We're sorry," said the controller, hesitating. "All entry docks are full. You'll have to redirect to Ongar. We'll send some guide crafts to meet you outside the orbit."

Ronny sighed and Raaychila crossed her arms. "Just go to the docking station, they'll make room," she said.

Within minutes, they came upon the six IIU guide crafts. Ronny slowed their ship as if to join them, then fired up all the booster engines and blew past them. Raaychila shook her head at the audacity of the IIU's efforts to thwart her visit.

They approached the IIU Space Station, a flying fortress anchored on one of Watico's moons. The station resembled a massive wheel, with the command deck in the center connected to an outer rim by twelve spokes. "We'll park there," said Ronny with a satisfied grin as they approached the dock. The radio transmission from the IIU had gone silent.

The vessel hovered into the docking bay and landed smoothly in an open space. "See," said Raaychila, "I knew they would make room." She and Ronny rose from their seats and stretched. The cockpit doors opened and three Watican bodyguards joined them. Raaychila could see out the window that a few IIU agents were jogging towards the vessel. Ronny pushed a button and the light above the back exit turned green as the door opened with a burst of air. They walked onto the ramp as the agents approached.

An IIU officer stood with his hands folded behind his back, grinning uneasily. "Greetings, Vinya Raaychila. Welcome to the IIU Station. As you can see, we've been very busy searching for your son. I trust you're here to receive news on Jeremy?"

"Yes. And I understand Ms. Fritz is being 'processed.' However, we want to speak with her immediately." Raaychila glanced at a video monitor as some IIU spacecraft lifted off and shot out of a hangar.

"My apologies, Vinya. Yes, Ms. Fritz has been detained ... but she is already being transported to Watico Castle. You just missed her, I'm afraid. We also have new intelligence about your son's whereabouts. But that information is classified—for your son's safety, you understand. The investigators who have that intelligence are also on their way to Watico Castle." The agent shrugged and then gestured to their space vessel.

"I'm afraid there's nothing more we can do at this time. Please accept our sincere apology for the gaps in communication. We've been working tirelessly to secure the return of your son. We'll refuel your ship and see you back out in orbit." More IIU agents flanked the officer, with one now beckoning a fuel cruiser across the hangar.

Raaychila narrowed her eyes. "How inconvenient that no information was available when I was on Watico, and no information is available now that I'm at your space station in person. If I didn't know better, I would think someone's hiding something from me."

"With all respect Vinya, the IIU is committed to full transparency with you and the Vor," said the officer, flashing her a toothy grin.

Just then, a robotic voice blared on the loudspeaker throughout the station: "Ms. Fritz, please report to flight deck 2020 for Earth. Flight deck 2020 leaving for Earth in twenty-five minutes. Earthbound, Flight deck 2020."

Raaychila blinked. "What's this? Ms. Fritz is going to Earth?!"

"She is not, Vinya," blurted the officer. "There must be a glitch in the automated system. Ms. Fritz has been detained and is going to—"

"Ms. Fritz, please board for Earthbound Flight 2020—"

"She's going to Watico!" yelled the officer.

"At this time, Ms. Fritz, destination Earth."

"Excuse me." Vinya Raaychila turned and dashed back up the ramp and into the cockpit of the Watican vessel, while Ronny continued to question the officer. The Vinya grabbed her phone and dialed Wantoro.

"Yes? Hello. Any news?" answered Wantoro.

"Ms. Fritz is going to Earth. There's some message on the intercom at the IIU dock about an Earthbound flight."

"What?"

Then a blast on the dock outside shook the Watican vessel, and Raaychila dropped her phone. There was shouting and gun fire. Raaychila ducked and looked out the cockpit door. Ronny and a Watican guard were retreating up the exit ramp, firing their guns behind them, and then dashing through the cabin towards the cockpit.

Raaychila slapped the button to close the back hatch, but two IIU agents slipped through the doors before they closed. A bullet tore through a Watican guard's head, splattering blood into the cockpit. Raaychila screamed. Ronny returned fire, catching both agents in the chest, and they dropped to the floor.

"We have to get out of here!" said Ronny, closing the cockpit door. Bullets ricocheted off the outside of the ship.

Raaychila rocked back and forth. "Hurry!"

Ronny flipped the start-up switches and the engines roared. Outside the cockpit there was a clunk, and they saw a movable staircase next to the front hatch. "Override code accepted," said the ship's computer, and the front hatch door opened.

Two IIU agents came up the steps with weapons drawn. Ronny deflected the barrel of one gun away from them, but the other fired. A bullet ripped up through Raaychila's cheek and she collapsed on the seat, gushing blood. Ronny pushed away the barrel of the agent's gun with one hand while firing two shots with the other, and the agents tumbled down the stairs. He slammed the hatch door lock and the door sealed shut. "Raaychila, stay with me!"

Shots continued to fire outside. Then a cannon blasted the side of the ship, tearing a hole in the cabin and shaking the craft violently. Ronny pressed the release button to free the front of the ship and then pulled the craft upright, simultaneously exerting pressure on Raaychila's bleeding cheek with his free hand. The ship lurched forward and shot out of the hangar into the atmosphere.

Raaychila, covered in blood and shaking all over, grabbed Ronny's hand.

"Stay with me," said Ronny. "I'll get you back to the castle!"

"Ronny, I..." Raaychila's voice gurgled and she gasped for breath.

"You're going into shock. I have to control the bleeding." Ronny took his uniform jacket off, ripped the sleeve, and wrapped the cloth around Raaychila's head.

"They... Jeremy!" mumbled Raaychila.

Ronny pulled his phone from his pocket and dialed Watico's Emergency Squad.

Raaychila tried to keep her eyes open. She shivered and gasped every time a dull sleep crept over her, her eyes rolling back. Sound began to fade.

CHAPTER 23

THE DEMON WITHIN

Jeremy struggled to break from his restraints, but the ropes held him to the table. He snarled and flung his head wildly about. The men closed in around him as the women pushed in from the outskirts for a closer look.

Minister Glibson splashed holy water onto Jeremy's face. "God arises; His enemies are scattered and those who hate Him flee before Him. As smoke is driven away, so are they driven; as wax melts before the fire, so the wicked perish at the presence of God."

The assembly chanted in unison, "Vade retro Satana."

"Let me go!" said Jeremy, still writhing in his restraints.

Minister Glibson continued, "We drive you from us, unclean spirits, all satanic powers, all infernal invaders, all wicked legions, assemblies and sects. In the Name and by the power of Our Lord, may you be snatched away and driven from the Church of God and from the souls made to the image and likeness of God and redeemed by the Precious Blood of the Divine Lamb!"

More holy water splashed onto Jeremy's face. Jeremy gnashed his teeth and cursed. The ties on his wrists were beginning to cut off circulation to his hands. Suddenly, Jeremy felt a surge of energy deep within his sternum. A blue spark shot up from his chest and his hair stood upright.

The crowd gasped and withdrew from the table. Minister Glibson splashed more holy water onto Jeremy and yelled, "Most cunning serpent, you shall no more dare to deceive the human race, persecute the Church, torment God's elect and sift them as wheat! God the Father commands you," more holy water. "God the Son commands you," another splash. "God the Holy Ghost commands you!"

"Vade retro Satana," answered the congregation.

Jeremy willed himself free and focused all his energy into his sternum, opening a gate there, from which electricity surged down his body. He concentrated despite the numbing pain that traveled up his arms. His sternum spewed blue sparks.

"I can see the demon!" yelled Henrietta, pushing towards the table. "Get out of my boy, devil!" Henrietta dug her fingernails into Jeremy's flesh, ripping down his arm. Jeremy screamed. A blue bolt arced from his chest and zapped Henrietta in the face, and she fell onto her back.

Minister Glibson splashed more holy water onto Jeremy as Bill and Bobby grabbed loose ply boards from the rafters. Jeremy snarled and shed sparks as he struggled. Bill dealt the first blow. The ply wood cracked onto Jeremy's shin. Then a board thudded on his chest, and he screamed. His body ached and burned, but somewhere in the back of his mind he heard a faint voice calling his name.

"Jeremy! They have Jeremy!" It was his mother. Jeremy could feel vibrations rippling through his body. He'd leave this place. He'd follow the voice, just as he had back on Findle. Jeremy tried to concentrate. He slowed his breath down. Another plank struck him across the face and he cried out. *Concentrate!* Jeremy took in another breath, exhaled, and his body rattled.

"Jeremy!"

Plywood thundered on the top of his head.

Jeremy was back behind the air, floating up through the tunnel that traveled through the purple Haze. "Mom?" Jeremy swam against the current of the tunnel and pushed through its membrane and into the swirling lavender. Soon, animals were drifting past him, towing their dead passengers.

"Jeremy, I tried to find you!"

Jeremy turned and saw a bear pulling his mother slowly through the Haze by a chord attached to her sternum. She was faded and translucent. The bear stopped and licked

Rachilla's cheek, which was gushing blood from a hole in the flesh.

Jeremy's eyes widened. He swam to her, weaving between animal spirits and their dead. "Mom? What happened!"

Raaychila looked at him and gasped. His body was covered in bruises and blood. "I'm sorry Jeremy. Have I died? Are you dead?"

"No! I'm just... I'm on Earth and, there's Mantel, and..." Jeremy felt a hollowness in his chest. He tried to embrace her. "No!"

Just before he could close his arms around her, the bear grunted and yanked Raaychila's chord, pulling her away. Then swarming around Jeremy was herd of animals and their dead passengers, and he jostled through the crowd after his mother, but no matter how hard he swam—like a dream where you are powerless to change the outcome—Raaychila grew fainter in the Haze, and then disappeared in the procession.

"Mom!"

Jeremy's body vibrated again. Underneath the folds in space where he now existed, there was a trace of awareness lingering outside the Haze. He kicked back and sideways and the purple disappeared. He opened his eyes and was back on the table in the Truist's shed.

The congregation encircled the table and was staring at him expectantly. Jeremy's body throbbed in a dozen places, and he felt sticky patches of blood coagulating on his skin. He had no energy left to struggle, to surge; he could only cry.

Minister Glibson raised his hands in the air. "Praise be to God!"

CHAPTER 24

THE WATICAN DEFENSE FORCE

Vor Wantoro sat at a table surrounded by advisors. He rubbed his temples. It had all happened so fast. "We'll follow the IIU. Dispatch the army. Call in the reserve."

Twenty men and women sat, unblinking, before the Vor, their hands clasped in front of them. Paintings of Vordin Chikalto charging into battle hung on the wall, seeming to cast echoes of war through the room.

"To Earth, sir? Do we have enough supplies for all our troops?"

"Of course we do, I've declared a state of emergency. The Assembly's already been voted in, and they'll rule in my stead. The people will get their democracy. We leave in two hours. The sooner we leave, the sooner this will all be over!"

"And Vinya Raaychila?" asked a hoarse voice.

Wantoro froze. Everyone waited in silence for his response. "She," he ran his hands through his hair and frowned, "comes with me." Wantoro strode out of the room and slammed the door behind him.

A Watican Defense Force comprised of twenty-five large crafts, each carrying twenty smaller crafts, shuttling three thousand soldiers, loomed on the horizon. The ships roared ahead, lining the sky with blue, purple, and pink streaks. Wantoro hoped to catch up with IIU forces within the next forty-two hours. If they could take any prisoners, they might be able to piece together a coherent narrative, beginning with the kidnapping of Jeremy, Maren, and Lyrna, and leading up to the attack on Raaychila and the Watican Royal Guard. The destination of the IIU and of Ms. Fritz was concluded to be Earth, though Wantoro couldn't begin to understand why.

Gillian and Mateo entered the parlor of the Watican Mothership through sliding glass doors. The room smelled strongly of lavender. "Wantoro, we're so sorry!" Gillian and Mateo rushed forward to offer their condolences. "Senseless," said Gillian. "This is all just so senseless."

Wantoro nodded. "Gillian, Mateo, we'll find our children. Raaychila," it pained him to say his wife's name, "remains in critical condition, but she's still with us."

"How long has she been in the coma?" asked Gillian in a soft voice.

"Nine hours, thirty-seven minutes." Wantoro sighed, and then turned away.

CHAPTER 25

LOCKED

The next three days, Jeremy was confined to the shed, shackled and chained to the back wall, his despair increasing hourly. He rarely saw sunlight and subsisted on water and potatoes. He had tried to escape, but his electricity was waning, unpredictable, and useless against the chains anyway. Worst of all, he couldn't summon enough energy to cross over into the Haze. According to Minister Gibson, there were still traces of the demon in Jeffrey, but it could be purged with a biblical amount of fasting and bodily discipline.

Jason approached the shed doors. Jeremy knew it was Jason because he always whistled the same song out of key. Jeremy cringed at a particularly shrill b-flat.

"Hey demon boy!" said Jason, opening the shed doors. "Ma's got some scraps of bacon left, thought she'd be nice and give you some of the fat. I told her she'd be better off usin' it to grease the pan." Jason flicked the clumps of bacon fat onto the floor by Jeremy's feet. Jeremy knelt on his knees, pulling his chains tighter. His hands couldn't reach the floor, but his mouth could get there with a stretch. Feeling very much like a dog, the smell of the bacon fat made him salivate.

"Hah! Not Ma's favorite no more, are you? You know it's my birthday next week? And I'm gonna eat my cake in front of you like this," Jason bent his head down so Jeremy could get a better look, and then obscenely licked his chops. "If you're good and don't start trouble, maybe I'll let you have a piece of my cake. Maybe. Probably not though."

At that moment, Bill arrived. He grabbed Jason by the arm. "Hey! How many times I gotta tell you to leave your brother be. Always in here harassing him. Did you give him the bacon?"

"Yeah, geez!" Jason pulled his arm back from his father and rubbed it. "If you care so much, why not let him back inside?"

"Come on, you!" Bill held the shed door open and Jason shuffled through. After the door closed, Bill said, "We're just waitin' to see if he's repented proper. Your Ma says we have to be patient," his voice trailed off. Jeremy heard the front porch door screech closed as they entered the house.

Jeremy closed his eyes and felt the hollow in the pit of his gut. How could he have lost both Maren and his mother? Jeremy lowered himself to the floor, hoping to lick up any extra bacon fat that he had missed.

A branch creaked outside. Jeremy lifted his head and stared at the shed doors.

"Lyrna want in."

"Lyrna!" said Jeremy. Her voice brought the first bit of happiness in some time.

"Jeremy!" A branch snapped. "Lyrna sorry. Lyrna chased. Back now." Lyrna quieted for a moment and then added, "Lyrna hungry!"

Jeremy pushed himself back up so that he slumped against the wall. "Sorry Lyrna, I don't have any more food. But can you help me out of here?"

Lyrna scratched at the door.

"It's locked. I think it's a pad lock. My hands and feet are in chains though and you'll need a key for that. Go see around the back. It looks like the chains feed to behind the shed."

Lyrna walked around to the back of the shed and then rapped on the wall. "Here?"

"Yes, what do you see?"

Lyrna growled and then ran off into the bushes. Jeremy heard the porch door swing open.

"Lyrna see Henrietta," whispered Lyrna. "Laundry."

A moment of silence passed and then the porch door screeched closed.

"Okay."

"So what do you see back there, around my chains? She does something to loosen or tighten them from back there," said Jeremy.

"Big lock on chain. Need key."

"Either Henrietta or Bill has it. You'll have to sneak into the house and find it."

Lyrna mewed. "But gun!"

"Tonight Henrietta will come out here to read to me. I'll ask her if she can loosen the chain on my left leg or something. You stay outside but follow her around the back to see what the key to the chain looks like."

"Attack? Get it!"

"No! Not yet, wait. I want you to follow her back inside and see where she keeps that key. Then go in when everyone's asleep and retrieve it. Can you do this?"

"Why wait?"

"Because if you attack her, we risk Bill and Jason coming outside." Jeremy imagined the board cracking against his chest, Lyrna's lifeless body, and then his mom floating in the Haze. Jeremy drew a ragged breath.

"Jeremy all right?"

"Lyrna, some terrible things have happened since you left. We can talk about it later. Just please be careful."

Later that night, Henrietta came to the shed. She tapped on the doors. "You okay in there, baby?"

"Could you come in?"

"'Course, what'd you think I was gonna do?" Henrietta opened the door and sat across from Jeremy in a green plastic lawn chair that had been brought in for devotions. She set down an oil lamp and straightened her crumpled dress, which featured teddy bears. "I brought you some milk, sweetie."

"Thank you," said Jeremy. Goat's milk had initially revolted him, but lately it tasted like ambrosia. Henrietta held out a pitcher to him. He leaned forward to catch the liquid in his mouth. After his first gulp, he spit some onto the floor, pulling his head back. "Why does it taste like that?"

Henrietta laughed, "Relax, only put some whiskey in it to help you sleep better is all. Now drink up. There's a lot and I don't want you to miss another drop." Henrietta tipped the pitcher to Jeremy and made a soft tutting sound with her lips.

Jeremy allowed the hot, bitter drink to flow into his mouth. It burned his throat and made his eyes water, but he knew he had to act appreciative to win her trust.

"Mother?" said Jeremy, as sweetly as he knew how. He shivered.

"Yes, baby?"

"My left foot hurts really bad. I can't pull it out as far as my right and I've been putting all this extra weight on it. It feels numb and tingly." Jeremy's eyes teared. "Please, could you please loosen it?"

"Oh, come now Jeffrey." Henrietta folded her arms across her chest and gave him a quick look over. She admired his changed demeanor. "Baby, that's how the whiskey's gonna help."

"Please?"

"Patience is a virtue. And we must endure trials and tribulations to strengthen us so evil don't get a foothold."

"My foot!" Jeremy sobbed softly and looked down at his left foot.

Henrietta bumbled up from her chair. "Oh, all right then. But no funny business!" She slapped him across the face with an open palm, and then again, leaving splotches of red on both of Jeremy's cheeks.

"Yes ma'am," said Jeremy, eyes downcast.

Henrietta leaned forward and kissed the top of his head. "That's my baby." She exited the shed and went around the back. Jeremy could hear the jingling of a key and the click of the lock. Within seconds, the chain slackened, and Jeremy found that he could pull his left foot forward. He wanted to leap, to bend and flex, but restrained himself. He allowed for five additional inches of foot space, just enough to treat himself to a decent stretch, but not enough to arouse any suspicions.

Henrietta ambled in and plopped back down onto her lawn chair. She studied Jeremy's extra leg room and smiled. "There, that good for you?"

"Yes, thank you."

Henrietta proceeded with devotions, choosing as her topic the story of Cain and Abel:

[1] Adam knew his wife Eve intimately, and she conceived and gave birth to Cain. She said, "I have had a male child with the LORD's help." [2] Then she also gave birth to his brother Abel. Now Abel became a shepherd of a flock, but Cain cultivated the land. [3] In the course of time Cain presented some of the land's produce as an offering to the LORD. [4] And Abel also presented an offering—some of the firstborn of his flock and their fat portions. The Lord had regard for Abel and his offering, [5] but He did not have regard for Cain and his offering. Cain was furious, and he was downcast. [6] Then the LORD said to Cain, "Why are you furious? And

why are you downcast? [7] If you do right, won't you be accepted? But if you do not do right, sin is crouching at the door. Its desire is for you, but you must master it." [8] Cain said to his brother Abel, "Let's go out to the field." And while they were in the field, Cain attacked his brother Abel and killed him. [9] Then the Lord said to Cain, "Where is your brother Abel?" "I know not," he replied. "Am I my brother's keeper?" [10] Then He said, "What have you done? Your brother's blood cries out to Me from the ground! [11] So now you are cursed from the ground that opened its mouth to receive your brother's blood you have shed. [12] If you work the land, it will never again give you its yield. You will be a restless wanderer on the earth." [13] But Cain answered the Lord, "My punishment is too great to bear! [14] Since You are banishing me today from the soil, and I must hide myself from Your presence and become a restless wanderer on the earth, whoever finds me will kill me." [15] Then the Lord replied to

him, "Therefore, whosoever slayeth Cain vengeance will be taken on him sevenfold." And the Lord set a Mark upon Cain, lest any finding him should kill him. [16]Then Cain went out from the Lord's presence and lived in the land of Nod, east of Eden.
— Genesis 4:1-16

Henrietta closed her Bible and stared at Jeremy. "Does this mean anything to you?" She studied his face.

Jeremy shook his head.

"Do right and you'll be accepted," was all she said, and it somehow didn't sound like her, but deeper, distorted. She rose from her seat and returned to the house. Jeremy, meanwhile, was beginning to feel nauseous.

CHAPTER 26

PIRATE

The fleet of IIU spaceships sped towards Earth with Watican forces at its heels. In the IIU Mothership, Ms. Fritz and Bentley sat at a table in the commander's lounge. A young IIU recruit sat before them, his mouth agape in admiration. Ms. Fritz turned the black orb over in her hands, contemplating its dark swirls. Bentley sat across from her, also admiring the communication device with his snake-like eyes.

Ms. Fritz brought the orb to her chest. "Bentley, I must commend our young comrade here for his excellent work disabling the satellites. It bought us precious time to fulfill our mission. Your resourcefulness has been noted."

The young recruit bowed his head in appreciation.

Ms. Fritz continued, "Mantel's servants know exactly where the Cajjez is located." She smiled and caressed the orb. "Wait until you see Mantel's powers."

"How does it work, exactly?" asked the young man, pointing to the orb.

"Oh, now you know I can't rightly explain it." She winked at Bentley.

Bentley crossed his arms and leaned back in his chair. "Indulge us. Jasmine said you let her hold it."

Ms. Fritz sighed. "I've been told that it operates through subtle vibrations—frequencies beyond what are detectable by instruments; that is, except by the instrument of a living being. The soul exists on these levels and continues there after bodily death. The substance inside this orb," Ms. Fritz shook the orb for emphasis, "is from the Haze, the place where the souls of the dead go before they're sorted to Heaven or Hell. The substance works as some type of conductor. This is our window into celestial affairs."

Bentley eyed the orb and licked his lips. "Tell our friend here about Mantel's promise." He leaned forward across the table, propping his head up with his hands.

The young recruit nodded. "I keep imagining this maze, and the possibilities it holds."

Ms. Fritz smiled. "Mantel's domain is a beautiful maze, where souls walk about in human form. They think, they drink, eat, love! Just as life is a myriad of choices, so is death. Mantel promises an everlasting, eternal life of choice. I've seen it, I've seen the harvested souls! What a fate, to remain individuated, to have free will forever! Mantel warns that if our soul joins God after we die, our individuality will be extinguished and we'll be doomed to live a life of selflessness. If we join Lucifer, we'll be forced into servitude and eternal pain. What we really want is to preserve life as we know it. If Mantel controls Jeremy, Mantel will gain unlimited access to the place where souls are sorted and he'll be able to bring more souls into his domain." Ms. Fritz frowned. "The current method of acquiring souls one by one is slow, tedious work. But imagine if we help his paradise grow. We'll have an honored place at his table!" Ms. Fritz held the orb up to Bentley and the new recruit. A swirl of purple emerged briefly on its black surface and then disappeared into its center.

An IIU officer marched into the lounge and stood at attention. Ms. Fritz, Bentley, and the young recruit turned to the officer, whose face was locked in a stone-cold expression.

"Watican forces are closer than expected. We're picking up some small spy crafts on our radar. We've spotted two so far, but we're certain there are more."

Ms. Fritz pushed up from the table, hiding the orb in the pocket of her robe. "So it's begun." She paced the room. "We'll have to attack. We have to drive them off. We can't have the Watican Royal Defense Force come to Earth. They'd ruin everything!"

Bentley looked up from under his bushy brow. "You don't think they'd actually follow us for five years, do you?"

"I do." Ms. Fritz recalled an image of Wantoro in her mind's eye. His face was resolute. "Some of our forces won't make it to Earth if we fight. But those who fight and die will be honored as martyrs and Mantel will know of their deeds. He will find their souls, mark me. We must have faith. If, no, *when* Mantel has Jeremy under his control, our forces, deceased or otherwise, will find their way to Mantel's Maze."

"So then we'll all die, is that what you're suggesting?" Bentley frowned.

"No, our ship and a few others will continue forward. The rest will hold them off. I'll leave it up to you to determine which ships join us."

Bentley massaged his chin. "First, I propose we send one of our interceptors to pirate one of their ships."

"We haven't the time for those games, Bentley!"

"Ms. Fritz, please. If we pirate one of their spy crafts, we can bring it back to Watico's Mothership and attempt to kidnap Wantoro."

"Now wait," Ms. Fritz's voice trailed off. "And you're aware that this is likely to be a suicide mission?"

"What else is turning around and fighting Watico's fleet? Besides, you forget our units are highly trained in subterfuge. And if we succeed, Wantoro could prove to be excellent leverage in securing Jeremy's allegiance."

Ms. Fritz smoothed her hair back and straightened her posture. "Very well, let's begin."

CHAPTER 27

SEVERANCE

The cool night air drifted in from a crack in the base of the shed, tickling Jeremy's feet. Outside, the drone of crickets continued. Jeremy focused on this, waiting for the pause of chirp song that would mark Lyrna's approach.

"Chirp, chirp, chirp," Jeremy babbled. His head felt like it weighed a ton. "Chirp," he sang, followed by "chirp!" an octave higher. The crickets quieted. *Oops*, thought Jeremy. A single cricket started up again but soon stopped. Jeremy tensed. Someone was approaching.

"Lyrna, key!" whispered Lyrna from behind the shed. Jeremy heard the lock jangle.

"Lyrna, pass the chains through the hole, I'll bring them through to my side. We have to try to do this quietly." Jeremy pulled the chains through as Lyrna fed them through the hole in the back of the shed.

"Chains all knotted," said Lyrna.

"It's okay, take your time," said Jeremy, his speech slurring from the whiskey Henrietta had put in his milk. The chain connecting his arm slackened and he pulled it through. Within minutes, Jeremy had collected all of the chains in his arms. He was now free to walk, though the chains were still attached to the shackles around his wrists and ankles. Jeremy shuffled to the door. "Lyrna, you have to figure out how to open this door. I think it's a pad lock." Jeremy leaned against the door, his head throbbing. "But be quiet."

Jeremy's pulse quickened as he heard Lyrna dragging a trashcan across the lawn to the shed door. "Come on, come on." The lock rattled and clicked and then the door opened.

Lyrna leapt into the air, then pranced around as a steady purr rumbled in her throat.

Jeremy gestured with his arms full of chains and smiled. "Thanks, Lyrna." He looked up at the house. The lights were still off. "Quick, back here." Jeremy shuffled to the back of the shed and used the final key to unlock his shackles. As he placed the instruments of his incarceration in a heap on the ground, relief washed over him. Jeremy pointed towards the woods. Lyrna nodded.

They picked their way slowly through the woods because Jeremy's head was reeling. His stomach gurgled and he knelt down in a patch of grass and vomited.

"Stinky!" mewed Lyrna.

"Sorry." Jeremy struggled to rise. "How far are we?"

"Feel okay?" asked Lyrna.

Jeremy slumped forward onto the cool grass and everything went black.

"Come! Come!" said Lyrna.

Jeremy awoke to find Lyrna pulling on his sleeve. "What?" Jeremy felt his head, which was still throbbing. "What happened?"

"Jeremy sleep."

Jeremy stood up and looked around him. "What? Not long, I hope!"

"Still close to house. Need move!"

"Right."

Jeremy looked behind him. In the moonlight, the roof of the cottage was still in sight, poking through the trees. Jeremy stumbled towards Lyrna. The two briefly continued on a path before opting for a more hidden route through the brush. The bushes and rocks slowed their pace. Jeremy tried to be quiet, but it was hard not to crunch leaves and snap twigs. As he was still unsteady from drinking Henrietta's special goat milk, he was certain he'd fall if he tried to run.

Jeremy and Lyrna at last drew close to a break in the woods where a narrow road cut through. Hope seemed tangible once more.

Then a rock struck Jeremy in the back of the neck. Baffled, Jeremy spun around.

"Stay right there." Jason emerged from behind a tree, a pistol in his hand. He motioned with his other hand and Adam came into view. Adam laughed sheepishly.

"Jason," said Jeremy coolly, "put the gun down."

"Nope! And I'll tell you what's goin' down. See, I snuck out with Adam and seen the shed was empty. I think to myself, I gotta tell Ma and Pa, but then I think—why not take care of the problem myself? Always thinkin' you're so special. You're a liar and a fraud." Jason stepped closer and pointed the pistol at Jeremy.

"See, I think you ain't done being humbled. I think you need a few more days of eating off the floor. You need to go back in your cage." Jason snickered and took another step forward. Adam followed his example. "So where's that get us?"

Jeremy stood as tall as he could. "I'm leaving and you're not going to stop me."

"Really?" Jason laughed again and brought himself face to face with Jeremy. "'Cause the way I see it is I got a gun. And I know how to use it. Got a pretty decent shot, too." Jason brought the gun up to Jeremy's face. "You're comin' with me."

Jeremy knew he couldn't go back to that house. The Truists would tie him down and beat him. *And Lyrna...*

"Watch out for that cat!" yelled Adam.

Lyrna growled and coiled her body tightly, ready to pounce. She bared her fangs at Jason.

"What, that thing? That's the first thing I'm gonna take care of." Jason aimed the gun at Lyrna and squeezed the trigger.

Jeremy leapt forward and barreled into Jason just as the trigger pressed down. The gun fired and the bullet hit a tree. Jason toppled to the ground and Jeremy fell on top of him, trying to wrestle the gun from his grasp. Adam dropped to the ground and hid behind a tree.

"You're comin' home!" yelled Jason.

Jeremy pried Jason's fingers off the grip as his other hand seized the barrel. The gun was now under his control. But Jason kept grabbing at it, and drew it closer to his chest. The muzzle now pointed up under Jason's chin. Jason narrowed his eyes and at that moment Jeremy saw in Jason a sad envy. Jason held the gun's muzzle and kicked Jeremy in the gut, and Jeremy could feel the gun slipping. He pulled. A loud bang rang out. Their eye contact continued for a moment, and Jason's lips curled into a faint smile of relief. Jason slumped to the ground. Blood gushed everywhere.

Adam sprang up screaming from behind the tree and ran away.

Jeremy's head spun. He had never seen so much blood. Blood on his arms, his shirt, his face. Everything felt warm and sticky. Jeremy fell forward and wept on the ground. Jason was dead. He wouldn't have a birthday party next week. He wouldn't grow up to be a man. Jason was blood, all blood. He had killed Jason. The grass was covered in Jason. Crows gathered overhead, cawing for Jason. Even the ants and beetles seemed to crawl up from the Earth for Jason.

Rising slowly from the ground, the world seemed altered. Jeremy beat his fists on the ground. Life felt heavy. Answers no longer flitted before him. He was alone and lost. Where was the angel? Where was God? Jeremy sobbed as he stumbled towards the open road. Maybe there *was* a demon inside him after all.

CHAPTER 28

CHAOS REIGNS

Wantoro massaged his temples. He let his hand caress Raaychila's, which lay folded across her chest. Her coma hadn't broken. Raaychila's eyes tensed, giving her a strained expression, but every now and then, the dimples in her cheeks would twitch and light up her face. From the small room where she was kept, one might forget the chaos just beyond the closed door.

Wantoro acted in haste to pursue the IIU. What else could he have done? If he had waited and calculated, it would already be too late. He couldn't stand to lose both Raaychila and Jeremy.

Wantoro's thought was interrupted by a deep boom, and then a rumble, which shook the floor and walls of the Watican Mothership. A siren blared over the speakers and red warning lights in the ceiling flashed.

The door opened and a woman with a narrow face stood before him, breathless. "Vor Wantoro, the IIU struck

161

our shields with a long-range missile. Sir, it seems they are trying to draw us into battle. Also, a Watican spy craft has returned with intelligence on the IIU."

"Yes, all right. Let's get the intelligence and see what's what." Wantoro gazed at Raaychila and squeezed her hand. "I'll find him, don't worry."

Outside Raaychila's chambers, spaceship personnel were crisscrossing and running to their stations. There was another boom and rumble as a second missile exploded against the Mothership's shield. Wantoro surveyed the scene, and knew he had to rally the troops. No Watican alive had ever been to war, including him. He pressed a button on his uniform, activating his microphone.

"Soldiers of Watico." His voice thundered over the speakers, and a hush fell over the ship. "In times of peace, service is easy. But war puts our mettle to the test. The people of Watico have entrusted us with a sacred duty. You have all sworn the oath. We are the sentinels who stand watch over our bold enterprise of peace, justice, and truth. We are the lions who guard the pride, righteous hunters styled before God, rejoined in fraternal state." Wantoro raised his fist in the air. "I call upon you now to fulfill your oath! We will prevail. Our shields are strong and our weapons are fearsome. These traitors will rue the day they tangled with Watico!" At that, the soldiers cheered, and took up their stations with renewed vigor.

"Vor Wantoro, that was an inspiring speech," said the woman with the narrow face. "Please come this way to receive the intelligence from our spy craft." And they walked down a long hallway. On a video monitor in the corridor, Wantoro saw an explosion out in space, away from the Mothership. *The Watican anti-missiles must have intercepted an IIU attack.* Wantoro turned the corner.

Past the rows of Watican soldiers sitting at blinking stations, two figures rushed towards Wantoro. Gillian and Mateo looked bedraggled. Gillian's makeup was smeared and Mateo's hair was patchy, as though chunks had been pulled out. "Wantoro!" cried Gillian, grabbing his hands. "I've heard they have news about Jeremy! They might know about Maren, too. We're coming with you!"

Together, they went down an elevator toward the lower flight deck. Gillian lowered her eyebrows. "Why didn't they just come to you?"

Wantoro shrugged. "Classified information."

At the bottom of the elevator was a short hallway ending with an airlock door that opened with a woosh. The party approached a small, V-shaped spy craft. Wantoro and his escort went up the ramp into the ship, followed by Gillian with Mateo at the rear.

Four men dressed in blue and gold Watican uniforms greeted the Vor and led him to the command center in the cockpit.

"Here's our intelligence, sir," said one of the soldiers, gesturing to a grid bearing an outline of numerous ships. "We have the location of the IIU fleet."

Wantoro shook his head in disbelief and ran a hand through his hair. "This is what you brought me here for? We already know the—" Then something cracked the back of Wantoro's skull, and everything went dark.

Jeremy Chikalto and the Hazy Souls

PART 2

Jeremy Chikalto and the Hazy Souls

CHAPTER 29

JACEY MOON

Maren, now twenty, tossed her head back and laughed. "I'm not taking a taxi home! I live three blocks away from cafe." A light drizzle filtered down through the clouds above downtown Manhattan. Maren brushed her blonde tresses from her face, put up her umbrella and started walking.

"Seriously Maren," yelled her friend, "your parents are millionaires, why not just take a taxi? It's raining!" Maren's friend, a short brunette in a too-tight mini dress, waved her arms. "I'll get us a cab! Come on."

"No thanks." Maren laughed.

"But I want to talk about the after party, Maren you have to go to the after party, I'm begging you!"

"We'll see. Honestly, I'm more excited that Craig was nominated for an award." Maren turned her back to her friend and continued walking.

After waking up in the back of an ambulance in New York City five years ago, Maren's life had completely transformed. She was diagnosed with post-traumatic amnesia, and soon after adopted by celebrities Janet and Craig Dern. Tonight her adoptive father might win the Velkin Award for Best Supporting Actor in a TV Drama.

Maren jogged up the stoop in front of her family's brownstone, went inside, and tossed her books in a heap onto the gilded sofa. Maren's adoptive mother, Janet, descended the winding staircase to greet her daughter, wearing only a towel. Her wide-set, brown eyes scanned Maren up and down.

"I know you can take care of yourself, you're a college girl, etc. But I still think there's a lot you can learn from me." Janet dusted her hands together, as though she were about to tackle some serious work. "I had Beatrix pull out some things for you to wear tonight. They're on the bed. Make sure to bring your purse and pack some makeup! I know how you like to go au natural, but you never know when the cameras will be on you. And your father's already spoken to Cindy about this season and they want you to have a small role. He can tell you more about it, but you have to be prepared!" Janet grabbed Maren by the shoulders. "Go! Start getting ready! We have four hours!"

Maren held her breath until Janet reached the top of the stairs, where she straightened a watercolor painting of a harbor. Maren shook her head. She'd get some reading done first and then dress. Four hours was far too much time to sit around feeling stiff in some undoubtedly uncomfortable dress.

Maren stretched out on the cushioned sofa, reading *Wuthering Heights* and sipping hot chocolate. She was about to set her cocoa on its coaster when a large black spider scuttled across the coffee table. Maren screamed and the family maid, Beatrix, rushed downstairs to see what was the matter.

"Spider!" shrieked Maren, accidentally spilling hot chocolate on the sofa and cream-colored carpet. "Kill it! Kill it!"

Beatrix laughed and collected the spider in a folded-up newspaper. "Good for the bugs," she said, walking towards the patio. She opened the sliding glass door and set the spider down in a potted plant.

"Ms. Maren, you really should start getting ready. I'll clean this." Beatrix made to spray the carpet with her carpet cleaner.

Maren shook her head. "No, no. I'll get this. My mess. If it were up to me, there'd be a spider carcass mashed into the carpet, too." She smiled and took the cleaning supplies from Beatrix.

At seven p.m. sharp, the limo pulled up to the wrought-iron gates of the Donegall Tower. The gates glided open, and the limo cruised down the drive. Maren admired the rose gardens and the cobblestone path that wound through the manicured grass to a small hot spring. Its emerald water bubbled and seethed, lavishing steam over the white rocks decorating its boundaries.

In the center of the estate stood a fifty-story tower with grand arches. After Maren, Craig, and Janet got out of the limo, a man in a black tuxedo led the family inside to the theater. White, yellow, and blue spotlights swirled down onto a polished maple stage in front of a velvet green backdrop. The Derns took their seats. A voice over the speakers introduced Ms. Betty Donegall, President of the National Academy of Television.

Ms. Donegall entered amidst applause. She smiled and waved as she stepped to the podium. "Hello and welcome to this year's Velkin Awards Ceremony, celebrating outstanding achievement in television. Please refill your glasses. The wine you're drinking is courtesy of Fallstap Vineyards. Also, don't hesitate to call on our waiters and you'll be served shortly. Tonight we'll be presenting awards in 30 categories; you'll find the list of awards and nominees in your program. But first, to kick off the ceremony, I would like to introduce a very special friend of mine, a young man with exceptional talents, Resident Artist at the Donegall Tower, Jacey Moon." Ms. Donegall smiled and glanced behind her. "Ahem, Jacey Moon!" she repeated, louder.

Maren exchanged glances with her adoptive parents and flipped through her program. The category for Best Supporting Actor in a TV Series was the third award of the evening. The lights dimmed and Maren folded her program on her lap, yielding herself to the opening performance.

A spotlight flashed on a young man as he emerged through the backstage doors wearing a white tux with blue trim. Soft music rose from the orchestra pit, a crescendo growing with each step the man took down a staircase. He was about Maren's age, maybe a little older. Arriving at the bottom of the staircase, he swung around the banister. His timing was impeccable, his every movement in sync with the band. A camera panned over him, casting his image on large television monitors throughout the amphitheater. His eyes were electric blue, and he winked as his tenor voice debuted, wooing the crowd. He started out quietly, sweeping around a sweet melody, but soon he was singing up the scale with growing intensity, the intricate pattern layering on itself, transposing higher, swelling, probing some universal mystery. *Wait.* Maren's jaw dropped. *Jeremy Chikalto?*

Suddenly the orchestra kicked up the tempo and Jacey Moon was singing a new tune, fast and spritely. He whipped off his tux jacket, revealing a silver-plated vest, and swung around a pole. Launching forward, he slid on his knees across the stage, only to backflip into an upright position. The crowd roared as he twirled and spun in time with the orchestra, all while singing, never missing a beat. Maren's heart fluttered. Was it really him? Who else could it be?

When he finished, he was met with a standing ovation. He didn't stay long on stage, instead bowing swiftly and running out the side doors. The ceremony continued, but Maren's mind was frozen in time. Last she saw Jeremy he was much shorter; surely five years wouldn't mature him quite so much. And yet, it looked just like him: the same electric blue eyes, boyish nose, and mischievous smile. Even the singing and dancing had his extravagant signature, although more mature, but it had to be Jeremy! Was it so crazy? Maren's hands trembled as she tried to recall her last moments with him.

Five years had passed since Ms. Fritz promised to take them to a restaurant on Findle. The IIU were there. A gun was against her head. Jeremy and Lyrna had tried to fight off the IIU, and then... blackness. Maren awoke in the back of an ambulance on Earth. That's all she could recall. Doctors told her she suffered from amnesia, likely after a traumatic event. The bruises on her shoulders certainly suggested a struggle. Maren eventually dropped her story, succumbing to the pressure of a sound medical explanation, but she never forgot where she came from and who she was. And here he was, the Cajjez, in New York City.

Maren felt someone grip her arm. She looked up at

the camera just above the stage and saw herself jump. Everyone was clapping. Maren clapped too. Looking to her left, she saw that her adoptive father was gone and was walking onto the stage. Maren, suddenly in the present, beamed.

"Thank you!" said Craig Dern, accepting the award for Best Actor in a TV Drama. "I can't begin to tell you how much this means to me. A special thanks to my loving wife, Janet, and to our lovely daughter, Maren, both of whom have given me tremendous support these past few years. And thanks to Martha Prestley for your direction and guidance–it's been such a pleasure working with you. And Becket, Becket you're a genius. Thanks to all my co-stars and to the studio, if it wasn't for you, I wouldn't be here. This is such a surprise, I really don't know what to say. Thanks to all my fans, this wouldn't be possible without you. Thank you all!" Craig lifted his award above his hand and shook it proudly. The music faded as he waltzed back to his seat.

Maren rushed forward to hug him. "Craig!"

Craig laughed as he took his seat.

"Congratulations!"

"Ssshh, okay! Let's, sshh!" Craig leaned back in his seat and wiped his brow with a folded white handkerchief. He laughed. Janet gave him one last pat on the back as the next introducers took their spots on the stage.

Maren's mind jumbled again. Between Craig winning the award and Jeremy Chikalto being in New York, she hardly knew how to feel. Her body trembled and her stomach fluttered as she scanned the audience.

The rest of the Awards Ceremony went by in a whirl. Soon, it was eleven p.m. and guests were filing out in droves.

"Craig, are we going to the after party?" Maren tugged Craig's coat, and then Janet's. "Are we going? Can we go, please?"

"Oh Maren, I don't know. It's getting late." Craig looked down from his towering height and frowned.

"Please? We have to go!"

Craig's mouth twitched into a smile and he laughed. "Of course! You think I wouldn't go to the after party? I have to introduce myself to Ms. Donegall and give my thanks."

"Your father's on the job, Maren. He's got to network," said Janet.

"Tough job, right?" Craig laughed again and led the way down through the aisles and back outside. He pointed to the hot spring and said, "Beautiful, isn't it? They say it just appeared on the property five years ago. Absolutely stunning." Maren and Janet agreed.

One of Ms. Donegall's bouncers redirected the family back inside, opened the stage doors, and led the party through to backstage. Dressing rooms lined the hallway and people were rushing back and forth.

A woman stood in the hallway, directing a few assistants who scurried away to do her bidding. When the Derns approached, she turned around and smiled, crinkling her nose under big, black-framed glasses, and tossed an aqua-marine scarf over her shoulder. "Mr. Dern, what an absolute pleasure. And congratulations." She took Craig by his hands and gave him air kisses on both cheeks.

Craig obliged her with his own air kisses. "Ms. Donegall, the pleasure's all mine. *The* most elegant awards ceremony I've ever seen. And please, call me Craig."

Ms. Donegall repeated this ritual with Janet and Maren, and then an assistant led them all to the ballroom.

In the ballroom the party was already in motion, with people dancing across the crimson carpet and chatting over hors d'oevres and drinks. The affair was bathed in soft light from crystal chandeliers. While Craig worked the room, Maren slipped nervously into a bar seat next to Janet and requested a Shirley Temple. The bartender smiled and slid the drink her way. Time was of the essence. She had to find Jeremy.

"Janet," said Maren, biting her lip. "Do you mind if I wander off a bit? I thought I saw someone I recognized earlier."

"No, of course. Enjoy yourself!" said Janet, relief in

her eyes. "I'm so happy to see you wanting to socialize. The dance floor looks fun!"

Maren smiled and made off with her Shirley Temple, scanning the crowd for the mysterious Jacey Moon.

She asked after him slowly at first, making her way from one likely go-between to the next. But the more she thought about it, she didn't know if he had a type of friend, per se. She had never met any of his friends before. As she recalled quite sadly, she might have been his only friend, and even that was a stretch. An hour ticked by and Maren was growing nervous. She'd have to approach the one person she knew to have contact with him: Ms. Donegall.

Maren's heart pounded as she got closer to the crowd surrounding Ms. Donegall. It was a thick crowd bursting with aggressive social climbers. Everyone wanted a piece of the hostess, who was in her element tonight, laughing and touching shoulders and making witty repartee. Maren realized that waiting patiently on the outskirts was not going to work.

"Excuse me, Ms. Donegall!" Nothing.

The famed Penelope Jada held Ms. Donegall's attention. Penelope had won an Oscar the previous year and was currently making tabloid headlines with her on-again off-again fling with singer-songwriter Marcus Hedger. The actress tossed her long, black hair, blocking Maren from Ms. Donegall's view.

Maren wriggled around to the left. Director George Q. Martinez elbowed her in the face. Maren bottled up her fists. "Ms. Donegall! Excuse me, Ms. Donegall!" Tears trickled down her cheeks as she bounced up and down. Now waving her arms, Maren shouted, "Ms. Donegall! Jacey Moon is in trouble! Jacey Moon!"

"What?" Ms. Donegall held up her hand and silenced those around her. She locked eyes with Maren. "What did you just say?"

Everyone turned to look at Maren. "Um," she hesitated. "Well, can I talk to you in private?"

Penelope Jada laughed and threw a nasty look at Maren.

"Yes," said Ms. Donegall to the shock of everyone surrounding her. Ms. Donegall separated herself from her admirers and pulled Maren aside. "What's wrong with Jacey?" she said in a husky voice.

Maren felt a lump forming in the back of her throat. "Well, see, I know him. He's Jeremy Chikalto—"

Ms. Donegall's eyes widened. "Ssh! Please keep it down, young lady! Now what's wrong with Jacey?"

"He, I need to speak with him. He knows me—"

"No, no, no," said Ms. Donegall, shaking her head. "No one goes near him unless I give permission."

"But can't he just see me? As soon as he sees me, he'll know why I've come."

"And why have you come?" said Ms. Donegall.

Maren's lips quivered. She couldn't imagine being this close to Jeremy and not speaking with him. She had so many questions. "Ms. Donegall, I beg you! The last I saw Jeremy or Jacey, I mean, was five years ago and I need to speak with him!"

"Which is exactly why you won't be speaking with Jacey! His name is Jacey!" Ms. Donegall turned away and was about to take a step when she bumped into none other than Jacey Moon. "Jacey!" she said, startled. Ms. Donegall patted down her hair and adjusted her aqua-marine scarf.

"Madame, I was looking all over for you," began Jacey. "Kirsten Azure and her party requested a private performance, and I told them I have off for the evening, but she insisted that you said that she–" Jacey's eyes rested for a second on Maren and his speech trailed off. Stupefied, he tried to concentrate on Ms. Donegall. "I'm sorry, that you said that she could–" He glanced back at Maren who was standing petrified beside Ms. Donegall. "I'm sorry," addressing Maren, "but do I know you from somewhere?"

"Jeremy?" Maren could hardly make the word come out.

Jeremy went quiet, his mouth slightly open. "Maren?" He laughed and flung his arms around her. "Maren! Where did you?" Jeremy took a step back to size her up. Long blonde ringlets fell over her slender frame, which was draped in pink satin, and her delicate face looked back at him in wonderment. "You're beautiful! How? You're not dead!"

"You're not dead!" said Maren, tears flowing down her cheeks.

"But—you're alive!" Jeremy began to wipe away his own tears, embracing her once more.

Ms. Donegall adjusted her scarf and cleared her throat. "Ahem! Jacey. JACEY!"

Jeremy ignored her.

"JACEY!" she snapped, finally getting a sideways glance from the Cajjez. "I don't think this is a good idea."

"Relax, she doesn't know."

"What don't I know?" said Maren.

"Nothing," said Jeremy.

"Jacey! Will you stop this insanity? Tell me what's going on." Ms. Donegall glared at Maren.

Maren unlocked herself from Jeremy's embrace. "What's going on? Is something going on?"

"Will both of you relax!" Jeremy did a small dance in place as he ran his fingers through his hair. "Maren, this is Ms. Donegall. This is her estate and I'm the Resident Artist here." Turning to Ms. Donegall, "And this is Maren Nononia. We go way back. We're childhood friends."

"I go by Maren Dern," whispered Maren.

"And I go by Jacey Moon, as I'm sure you've heard." Jeremy bit his lip.

"Why Jacey Moon?"

"Because—"

"Jacey!" said Ms. Donegall, pulling him back by the shoulder.

Jeremy stumbled. After recovering his balance, he brushed Ms. Donegall's hand off his shoulder. "Relax. She doesn't know about that." Jeremy fixed his gaze on Maren. "And Maren, I can assure you, is smart enough not to ask about what 'that' is because it's obviously making you uneasy and it's really not necessary to inquire about at this time." Jeremy turned back to Ms. Donegall. "Maren, of all people, can best understand why I might be incognito without having to know the exact circumstances. I suspect that she is too, which is why, Ms. Donegall, you have absolutely nothing to worry about." He smiled.

Ms. Donegall sighed. She squinted through her big, black-framed glasses as she looked Maren up and down. She might have passed as a model if it weren't for her awkward gait and hunched shoulders.

Maren held her breath, and at last said, "It's true, Ms. Donegall. I won't speak a word of anything."

"Mmhm," said Ms. Donegall, hardly convinced.

"Hello, Ms. Donegall. I hope my daughter Maren's not taking up too much of your time." Craig and Janet Dern moved in beside Maren, wine glasses in their hands.

"We were looking all over for you, Maren. We're going to head out soon," said Janet. "And this must be Jacey Moon? A pleasure!" Janet shook Jeremy's hand and Craig did the same.

"Great show tonight, Mr. Moon. I see you've made an impression on our Maren." Craig smiled and winked at Maren.

Maren blushed. "Janet, Craig, can I just have a moment with Jacey?"

"Sure," Craig and Janet exchanged glances and laughed.

"I'll be right back with her," said Jeremy, grinning at a flustered Ms. Donegall.

Jeremy led Maren to his private loft on the top floor. Maren enjoyed the view from the window overlooking the city. The room was very Jeremy Chikalto, full of abstract sculptures, paintings, and jewels spilling out of crystal bowls.

"How did you get all this?" said Maren, looking around in awe.

"You're gorgeous," replied Jeremy. He leaned forward and stroked her cheek.

Maren stepped back. "Jeremy? But seriously, how did you get this?" Maren felt a hot flash spread across her cheeks and forehead.

Jeremy plopped down on his silk bedspread. "Because people like me, Maren. Gifts, they're all gifts." He gestured to the jewels.

"Maren!" mewed Lyrna from behind the dresser. Lyrna raced forward and leapt into Maren's arms. Maren giggled and hugged the purring fizdruft. "Oh, Lyrna! I missed you."

"I was wondering when Lyrna would wake up," said Jeremy, laughing.

"She's gotten so big!" said Maren.

"I still can't believe we've been living so close to one another." Jeremy gazed out his bed-side window. "Maren, what happened after I lost you in the Haze?"

"I'm sorry, the Haze?" said Maren, frowning.

"That's what I call the other place. The dead are there, and animals pull them by astral chords. It's purple and cloudy, sometimes mixed with other colors. It's like swimming through a thick, cool vapor." Jeremy spread his hands out in front of him and painted a picture in the air.

Maren blinked.

"Okay," said Jeremy slowly, "so then what *do* you remember?"

"That Ms. Fritz and the IIU were going to *kill* me and then there was blackness followed by light. I woke up in the back of an ambulance with an oxygen mask over my face. I was cold and had blue fingertips. The paramedics said I almost suffocated. Then I find out I'm on Earth!" Maren pulled at her hair. "Please tell me you know what happened? Did Ms. Fritz knock us out? How did she get us here?"

"Ms. Fritz didn't get us here, Maren. I brought us here."

"But then... How?" Maren shook her head.

"The Haze. Nobody can breathe in the Haze except for me." Jeremy lay back on his bed. "I've tried to go back, but I don't know how to enter or exit properly. I don't want to leave Lyrna behind, plus I'm not even sure where I'm going." He paused. "Besides, there's nothing there but death." Jeremy thought of his mother.

"What?"

Jeremy studied Maren, her face equal parts hope and fear. "I can go behind the air and it's full of spirits. Like I said, it's purple and–"

Maren closed her eyes and tried to concentrate. "Wait. Just wait a second."

"Okay." Jeremy got up and walked over to Maren. He wrapped his arms around her. "I can talk about other things, I just thought this was important."

"Jeremy!" Maren pushed him away. "Have you ever heard of personal space? Seriously!"

"It was an innocent hug?"

Maren walked over to the dresser. She leaned against it and began to cry. "I feel like I'm seeing a ghost!" Maren buried her face in her hands.

"Well maybe I am a ghost."

"You were saying something about an angel before we left," said Maren from behind her hands. She pulled her hands down off her face and stared at Jeremy. "That's what you told me before we came to Earth, right? That an angel talked to you?"

"Yes. Something talked to me."

"And then there's something else." Maren blushed. "I remember reading your diary once, not much of it. You wrote about the air twitching and how you put your hand behind it. Something..."

"Ah, so you did read my journal!" Jeremy smiled. "I caught you in your naughty act. It was before the Watican Awards Ceremony."

Maren rubbed her eyes and sniffled, looking out the window. Limos were pulling out of the parking lot in droves.

"Listen, I'll explain later. Right now, I just need some way of contacting you in the future. What's your number and address?" Jeremy grabbed a sheet of paper and a pen from his drawer.

Maren wrung her dress with her hands. "212-041-1810, 467 Cardiff Lane, New York, New York. And I know where you–"

"Don't come here looking for me," said Jeremy.

Maren froze like a deer in headlights.

"I just mean, there are better places for us to get together." Jeremy smiled. "I've missed you so much."

There was a knock on the door. Jeremy got up and looked through the peep hole, sighed, and opened the door.

"I'm here to—"

"Yes, yes," Jeremy waved off the butler. "All right, Maren, it was really good to see you."

"So?" Maren collected her pocketbook and gave Lyrna one last pet before Jeremy hurried her out the door. "I guess we'll meet again soon, Jeremy?"

"Jacey. Of course, Miss Nononia."

The butler escorted her away as Jeremy shut the door.

CHAPTER 30

TOUCH DOWN

Wantoro pressed his forehead against a window. Five years of imprisonment aboard the Intergalactic Intelligence Unit Mothership had given him a rugged, disheveled look and he hardly recognized his own reflection. White fluffy clouds gave way to an expansive blue sky. Within seconds, the cloaked spacecraft landed silently in an enormous cornfield on Earth. IIU personal unloaded the supplies and prisoners, escorting Wantoro, Gillian, and Mateo to a clearing where the corn stalks already lay withered and trampled.

"Welcome to Earth, Vor Wantoro," said Ms. Fritz. IIU General Bentley narrowed his lizard-like eyes and shoved Wantoro forward. Wantoro said nothing and scanned the horizon. Ever since being captured, he, Gillian and Mateo had been promised a reunion with their children. This thought alone fueled Wantoro's subservience.

IIU henchmen Jasmine and Drew pointed their guns at Wantoro's back.

"I thought we were past this," said Wantoro. "Lower your weapons."

Bentley snickered and called to Ms. Fritz. "You think we'll be there by nightfall?"

"Yes, for sure." Ms. Fritz led the group over a hill to an old, rusty windmill, and stood in its shade.

"Where are our children and when will we see them?" demanded Mateo. The four-year journey had stripped him of weight and good humor.

"My dear Mateo," said Ms. Fritz, grinning. "Have some water." She handed each of the prisoners bottled water. "You'll see your children as promised. Have we not been civil to you? Bentley, they're ungrateful, don't you think?"

"If they only knew," said Jasmine, "they'd be thankful. You should be proud to play such a central role in Mantel's grand scheme."

"Hush, Jasmine." Ms. Fritz examined Wantoro, Gillian, and Mateo. "You'd all be a lot healthier if you'd just stop worrying."

Gillian glowered at Ms. Fritz. "We'd stop worrying if you'd be forthcoming with us. What business do our children have on Earth? Who is Mantel?"

Ms. Fritz ran her fingernails across the side of the windmill, sending red paint chips fluttering to the ground. "I'm sorry to say, Gillian, but your child Maren has no business being here. She's only a tag along. It's Jeremy we're interested in."

Gillian gnashed her teeth.

Ms. Fritz laughed. "Perhaps it's not water you're wanting, Gillian. Should we mix a cocktail for you?"

"I'd like that actually," snapped Gillian.

"Silence!" Ms. Fritz slicked her hair back. "Bentley, we'll only be taking a few select IIU members with us, so have them ready in ten minutes. Send the rest to the Manor. Mantel's servants await their arrival. As for us," Ms. Fritz pulled out a map and dangled it in front of the prisoners, "we'll be taking a taxi to New York City. Stay close and keep quiet if you want to see your children."

Chapter 31

Memories Past

The limo dropped Maren and her Earth parents off in front of their brownstone. A crisp night breeze brushed their cheeks as they walked up the steps to the front door.

"Some night," said Craig as he entered a code into the security system. Janet yawned. Maren remained quiet.

Once inside the foyer, Janet turned to Maren. "So are you going to tell us about that beautiful boy who swept you off your feet?" She laughed and nudged Maren. "He had amazing eyes."

"Cajjez Jeremy did *not* sweep me off my feet." Maren frowned and fussed with her jacket buttons.

"Cajjez who?" said Janet, knitting her eyebrows together.

"Jeremy Chikalto."

"Is he, is Jeremy Chikalto the friend you recognized earlier?"

Maren imagined running upstairs and locking herself in her room. She had a lot to process. "Yes. I'm really tired."

"You look upset," said Craig. "I thought his name was Jacey Moon."

"Yes well, I mean Jacey Moon."

Janet exchanged worried glances with Craig. "So he has two names?"

"Stage name, perhaps," said Craig.

"No. Maybe. I don't know."

"Is everything all right? Did he try to do something to you?"

"No! It's not like that, we've known each other since we were kids! I'm sorry, I just have a lot on my mind." Maren clenched her purse to her chest and covered her face with her other hand. She sped up the stairs, through the hallway, and into her room, shutting the door behind her.

Craig and Janet stared at each other across the dining room table for a long time. Maren hadn't been able to remember anything before the night she was admitted to the hospital five years ago. She had been found unconscious on the side of the road in New York City. When Maren regained consciousness, she couldn't account for her whereabouts and there was no record of her name or birth in the social security database. Doctors believed she suffered from amnesia likely caused by a traumatic event. Bruises on her arms and wrists suggested there was a struggle. After ending up in the foster care system, she met the Derns, who adopted her a year later.

"What do you think this means?" Janet reached across the table and clasped Craig's hands. "Do you think she's getting her memories back?"

"I guess so, she said she knew Jacey Moon as a child."

"But she was calling him Jeremy Chikalto."

"Jeremy Chikalto," said Craig slowly, sounding out each letter. "We should contact the doctor. We have to figure out what triggered the memory. We'll put everything in writing that happened this evening." Craig rose from his seat and found a pad of paper and a pen.

"Craig, let's calm down. It's been a long evening. We can ask Maren about it in the morning."

"What if he hurt her? What if that triggered her memory?" Craig scribbled the name "Jeremy Chikalto" down on the pad of paper.

"Okay, and what if we've all had too much to drink. You saw the place, Maren could have gotten alcohol easily. Kids do stupid things. Let's leave her alone tonight and we'll ask her about it in the morning."

"Janet, you're making excuses. This could be serious. I'm calling the doctor. You know what? I want a background check done on Jeremy Chikalto. I'm calling Steve."

"Craig, it's two in the morning! This is insane."

"What if he hurt her? Or, okay, maybe he didn't hurt her, but what if he's connected somehow to Maren's past?" Craig jabbed a finger in the direction of Maren's room. She was wailing. He picked up the phone and was about to dial.

"Tomorrow, Craig." Janet placed her hand on top of his and guided the phone back to its charger.

CHAPTER 32

ENCHAINED

There was a knock on the door. Lyrna hissed and ran under the bed. "Jacey, so sorry to interrupt. Ms. Donegall requests a word with you in her room."

"Of course," said Jeremy. He donned his robe and exited the room.

"Yes, Madame?" said Jeremy as he entered Ms. Donegall's chambers. She was pacing in front of her gilded vanity table.

"Don't play sweet with me, Jacey!" Ms. Donegall swept past Jeremy and yanked the crystal necklace off his neck. He gasped as the clasp pinched his skin and then snapped. She shoved the necklace into her bra. "Who is this Maren Dern? I've had her checked out and she's had amnesia, too?" She snorted. "Do you know how much I've risked to keep you safe? And this is how you repay me?"

"I told you earlier, she doesn't know about my past."

"Apparently I don't either. I could lose it all, you know! Everything I've worked so hard for, my estate, my career! And all for you. Aiding and abetting a murderer. That's the headline that will ruin me." Ms. Donegall slapped Jeremy's cheek with the back of her hand and then shoved him. He fell back into a love sofa. "Don't associate with anyone from your past. You have all that you need here."

"I barely knew her," he lied. "I'm just memorable is all."

"Remember what would happen to you in prison. It'll be far worse than your experience with the Truists. You killed a young boy. Say his name."

"Jason Truist. I killed Jason Truist."

"That's right, now sing me to sleep."

Jeremy looked down. "I'll need some water. I'm thirsty."

"Later. Now sing." Ms. Donegall opened the canopy to her bed and climbed in. She put on her night cap, a gray streak of hair falling across her forehead, and closed her eyes.

Jeremy felt for the absent necklace around his neck and sighed.

The crow wandered in search of a pyre
to char its dread in the moonless air.
And the volcanos burned as beacons,
the habitations of the dead,

dwelling deep in the gloom,
burning as the flames of a watchfire.

Jeremy returned to his room and called Lyrna. She crept out from under the bed and sat on his lap. "We could sneak Maren in here."

"No, we leave," pleaded Lyrna.

"Maren would love it here. I could get curtains and we'll partition the room. Ms. Donegall couldn't know, of course, she'd never have it. The place is small, but it's comparable to life in the Farmoore Galaxy."

"Not."

"Well, what I mean is, I'm treated like royalty."

"Like fool."

"Do fools get jewelry? Anything they want to eat? Clothes?"

"Like, like doll!"

"Really? Do dolls get those things?"

"Sing and dance like fool!"

"Shut up, Lyrna."

Lyrna jumped down from his lap and ran under the bed. "Buys you."

"Ms. Donegall protects me." Jeremy got down on the floor and peered under the bed.

Lyrna stared.

"I have Maren's address. I'll get her tonight." Jeremy rummaged in his closet and found a black ski mask. Then he lifted up a loose floorboard and pulled out a long rope. He tied it to the heater beside the window, pulling the knot taut to make sure it would hold. "When I get to the stairs next to the building, pull the rope up. Do it quickly. I'll be back in like two hours." Jeremy grabbed the note with Maren's address and a silver necklace with an emerald teardrop pendant. "She'll like this."

Chapter 33

At the Gates

It was the dead of night, but New York City was lively as ever. Wantoro watched the menagerie of people and lights from the window of a taxi cab. Would he find his son here? His brain felt as scattered as the city streets.

Bentley sat in the front passenger seat, sharing an awkward silence with the driver, while Wantoro shared the back seat with Gillian and Mateo, an arrangement too snug for a man accustomed to his own quarters, even as a prisoner. Mateo had insisted on the middle seat so Gillian could have a window, which meant that Mateo's thigh was touching Wantoro's, and no matter how much he squeezed toward the door, Wantoro could not stop this excruciating intimacy.

Gillian clung to her husband. "What do you suppose Maren looks like now? Do you think we'll recognize her?"

"I'm sure she looks like you, stunningly beautiful."

"Oh, Mateo." Gillian went to slap his gut but instead smiled at its absence. "You really should try to keep the weight off this time."

"If duck, lamb, and cannolis want in, they may enter."

Wantoro rolled his eyes and smiled despite himself. At least the Nononias had each other. Wantoro dreaded breaking the news of Raaychila's coma to Jeremy. He racked his brain for ways to delay this conversation, but no solution presented itself. More than anything, though, he yearned to see his son alive and well.

In the cab ahead of them, Ms. Fritz could barely contain her excitement. Every block or so, she would redo her bun, taking her hair out of its rigid coil only to recoil it more rigidly. She clapped her hands. "Oh Jasmine, Mantel is close. Can you feel it?" The driver gave her a raised eyebrow.

As they continued on, traffic thinned out and they came to a high stone wall. "Here we are," said Ms. Fritz, and the cabs slowed to a stop. As they climbed out of the cab, Ms. Fritz paid the exact amount of Earth dollars displayed on the meter. She didn't notice the driver's dirty look as he pulled away. They stood before the wrought-iron gates of the Donegall Tower.

"Nice place," said Jasmine. "Pretty tight security, I imagine?"

"Not a problem," said Ms. Fritz. She walked to a tree just left of the entrance and inserted her hand into a hollow, extracting a set of keys. Next, she entered a code into the security box. A speaker buzzed her in as she opened the gates with her key.

CHAPTER 34

THE BREAK-IN

Jeremy stood across the street from 467 Cardiff Lane, the brownstone townhouse where Maren's family lived. He looked up and down the street to make sure he was alone, and then pulled his black ski mask over his face before crossing the street. His dark, blue-black jeans and navy blue sweater may have helped him blend in with the city's nightscape, except for a distinct white fur paw pad that was stitched onto his breast pocket. ("I have to maintain some signature pizzazz, Lyrna," he'd protested when choosing his ensemble.)

The entrance to the house was blocked with a barred metal door in front of the original wood doors. It was 3:30 a.m. He *could* wait until morning, but where's the fun in that? Jeremy reached up to the barred metal door and palmed the electronic security box.

Concentrate. Jeremy closed his eyes and slowed his breathing. He drifted between the physical plane and the

Haze. A current flowed into his hand, and electricity surged out and fried the security box. Smoke rose from the plastic casing, and he wondered briefly if this was a bad idea. *Nah, they have money to replace it.* Jeremy adjusted his ski mask and opened the barred door.

Now for the wood doors. He would need to be stealthy. Jeremy took his shoes off and put them in his bag. Next, he scrounged in his pockets for potential lock picks and settled on a credit card. He double checked the street, and was still alone. Jeremy slipped the credit card between the doors, easily pushing the bolt back into its socket. *No deadbolt? They're just inviting burglary.*

Jeremy eased open the door and crept into the foyer, his socks barely audible on the tile. He padded up a spiral staircase and into a hallway with a closed bedroom door. He heard Maren sobbing. He took a deep breath and burst into the room. Maren was laying on her bed facing the wall, and yelped at the sound of the intrusion, but Jeremy immediately stifled her mouth with his hand. Jeremy unmasked himself, poked his head around her shoulder, and laughed.

"Come with me," Jeremy whispered. He hugged her and pulled her to her feet.

"Jeremy, what is wrong with you!"

Jeremy pulled the mask back over his face and hoisted Maren over his shoulder.

"Jeremy, put me down!" Maren kicked and smacked him on the back.

"Quiet!" Jeremy rushed through the house with surprisingly little noise, Maren slung over his shoulder. After sliding out the front door, he set her down on the stoop and eased the door shut. He took his shoes from out of his bag and put them back on. Maren shivered and tried to cross her arms, but Jeremy grabbed her hand and led her recklessly down the front steps and onto the sidewalk. They jogged down the block until Maren pulled them to a halt, catching her breath. In the distance, headlights approached the intersection.

"What was that about! You could have just called?"

Jeremy took off his mask. "I thought this would be more fun." He shrugged.

"You kidnapped me! What if someone calls the police? So many reasons *not* to do whatever it is you just did."

"Hey, let's just keep going. It's not safe here."

Maren sighed. "Fine."

The two ran down the street together for some time past rows of townhouses, a playground, and a Thai restaurant, dodging the odd late-night pedestrian. At last they slowed.

Jeremy stretched his arms overhead. "What a rush."

"Can you tell me what's going on?" Maren brushed her hair off her face.

"I wanted to take you to my place. I'm not allowed out during the day, or during the night for that matter, but I do enjoy my great escapes." He smiled.

"You broke into my house. What if my parents heard you?"

"Your parents?" Jeremy frowned. "You mean that older couple you came to the party with?"

Maren began pacing. "They adopted me and consider me to be their daughter. If they realize I'm missing, they're going to call the police!"

"Listen, Maren, can you stop drawing attention to yourself? I'm trying to keep a low profile." Jeremy looked around sheepishly and stuck his hands in his pockets.

"Oh, because you've been so covert!"

Jeremy frowned.

"My house has cameras! Didn't you just give a performance for the Velkin Awards Ceremony? That's just like you, Jeremy. You haven't changed one bit."

"Maren, I'm sorry." Jeremy's eyes followed a police car that had sped around the corner. He looked back at Maren. "Cute pajamas."

Maren looked down. She was wearing her yellow chick fleece pajamas. "Okay," she said, taking a deep breath as another police car sped by. "I can hang out with you for an hour, but then we're going to have to clean up your mess."

"Thank you, Maren, that's very matronly of you." Jeremy started walking again.

Jeremy and Maren arrived at the back entrance of the Donegall Tower and Jeremy typed in the security code and opened the gates with his key. They walked along the cobblestone path past the gardens.

"You'd never think there was a party here only a few hours ago," said Maren, staring off into the distance at the pristine property.

"Ms. Donegall wouldn't have it any other way."

"Do you like her?" asked Maren.

Jeremy kicked a stone. "No."

"But she is your Earth mother?"

"No. I'm the Resident Artist here. She took me in about five years ago. Loves me, of course. Probably too much."

"What happened to you before then?"

"I robbed a family of something. I'm hiding out."

"Did you use your ski mask?" Maren smiled.

"No." Jeremy paused in front of a flowerbed of yellow jasmine. In another week they'd reach full bloom. "I almost forgot." Jeremy shuffled through his pockets and pulled out the silver necklace with the emerald teardrop pendant. He presented it to Maren. She smiled.

"Where did you get this? One of your gifted jewels?"

"Yes, but it's made for a lady." Jeremy watched eagerly as she clasped it around her neck. "Doesn't it make you feel good?"

Maren sighed. "Yes, I suppose it does bring back memories."

"Luxury makes me happy sometimes, you know? It reminds me of being on Watico."

Maren stepped off the path and admired a rose bush. Its soft, pink petals had collected dew. She caught a whiff of its perfume. "Jeremy, what was it like to have the entire Farmoore Galaxy at your beck and call?"

Jeremy laughed and joined her by the rose bush. "It wasn't like that. People hated me."

"They did not."

"They did."

Maren knew he was right. Jeremy was unpopular. But everyone had a high opinion of his art, and young girls, especially, enjoyed his looks.

"Why do you think people disliked you?" Maren avoided his eyes.

"Because I'm insecure, capricious, selfish. Crazy." Jeremy shrugged.

"Well at least you're capable of moments of clarity. But it turns out you were always telling the truth." Maren smiled at Jeremy and took to the path again.

"Did you want to head inside or continue to the front of the property?" Jeremy caught up to her and resisted the urge to reach for her hand.

"Do you think you can bring us back?" Maren's face lost the glow of the gardens. "I can watch Lyrna if you're afraid to leave her alone and you can, um, practice going to the Haze. We have to try, right?"

"Of course." How could Jeremy effectively communicate the horror and strangeness of that place? Of the twists and turns in space and his inability to navigate it? He knew he must try. There was a heavy awareness that tugged at his brain whenever he crossed over, like he could feel traces of familiarity. He could yield himself to those paths and be led, but to where, he didn't know.

CHAPTER 35

WANTED

Maren wasn't answering her phone. Craig Dern dialed 911.

"State your name and location."

"Craig Dern. 467 Cardiff Lane, New York, NY."

"What's the problem, sir?"

"My house was broken into and someone kidnapped my daughter, Maren Dern! His name was Jeremy Chikalto or Jacey Moon! He took my daughter!"

"Sir, please calm down. Did you see the suspect?"

"I know Chief Browning. Tell him—tell him Craig Dern needs help! I have this Jacey guy on my security video but he's wearing a mask. I was in my bedroom. He's a young man, around eighteen, twenty years old, and I saw him at the Donegall Tower last night. He's a dancer, a singer. He went by the name Jacey Moon, but my daughter mentioned that he's Jeremy Chikalto. He has blondish, brownish hair, he's tall, around six foot and athletic build."

The operator typed something into his computer. "Jeremy Chikalto. We have him on file linked to a missing person report. Wait, I'm seeing something else in his file. He's considered dangerous. At the Donegall Tower, you said?"

Craig stood up, knocking his chair back. "Dangerous?!"

CHAPTER 36

THE HOT SPRING

Lyrna lay on the window ledge staring at a light outside. An hour had passed and Jeremy hadn't returned. She jumped down and busied herself with her food dish—halibut garnished with rosemary—when she heard a scream from down the hallway.

"Jacey! Jacey! Get up! The police are looking for you! Jacey!"

Sirens wailed in the distance as footsteps came closer to the room. Lyrna puffed and jumped back up on the window ledge. Three police cars skidded around the street corner towards the Donegall Tower. Lyrna mewed and ran the length of the room, not knowing quite what to do. She felt helpless. She gave one last mew and leapt out the window, jumping from window ledge to drain spout to window ledge, her claws scratching metal and brick in her descent. She'd have to find Jeremy.

After reaching the ground, Lyrna bounded along the cobblestone path towards a garden pavilion, planning to climb onto its roof, leap into a tree, and then drop from a branch onto the exterior wall. On the way to the pavilion, though, she passed the hot spring, a thing that always raised her hackles and was definitely a bad bad. The stinking green pool bubbled and frothed before her. Then a shadow fell on the pool, and Lyrna heard a familiar voice.

"Look who it is! My favorite pet. Lovely little creature, this fizdruft." Lyrna spun around to see Ms. Fritz hovering over the hot spring. The IIU, Wantoro, Gillian, and Mateo emerged from behind a bush. "Where's Jeremy?"

"Lyrna!" Wantoro jerked forward but was held back by the IIU.

Lyrna puffed and hissed. "Wantoro?"

"Lyrna," shouted Wantoro. "Where is my son? Is he here?"

"And Maren!" cried Gillian.

Ms. Fritz smiled. "Excellent question Wantoro. Tell us, fizdruft, where is Jeremy?"

Lyrna growled.

"But wait, here's the man of the hour, and what a fine young man!" Ms. Fritz clapped her hands together and laughed as Jeremy emerged from the side of the Donegall Tower, following along the cobblestone path. He was tall now with a boyishly handsome face and a trim build. His large eyes flashed in the moonlight. Maren followed Jeremy, thin with wavy blonde hair and sharp cheekbones. They were laughing and talking, but stopped abruptly when they saw the others.

They locked eyes with their parents. "Father?" Jeremy stumbled forward.

Bentley raised his weapon. "I hate to interrupt this happy reunion, but let me make something clear. This is why you should do as we say." He aimed his gun at a small shrub and shot a conical stream of fire, igniting the shrub and quickly burning it into a pile of ashes.

"Incinerator. Very dangerous." Bentley narrowed his eyes, stepped forward, and pointed the weapon at Maren.

"People, please. I know things are heating up, but let's proceed in an orderly fashion," said Ms. Fritz, disappointed when her pun didn't defuse the tension. "Okay Bentley, you can lower your weapon." Bentley lowered his weapon slightly, but it was still pointed at Maren. Ms. Fritz continued, trying to ignore the insubordination. Jeremy stared at Bentley's hand.

"Jeremy, Maren, as you can see we've brought your parents. Oh, joy. But Jeremy, you didn't follow my instructions to seek out Mantel. You always did have a problem with attention and I guess gallivanting around Manhattan was just too tempting. But here is the way to Mantel now, right in front of us." Ms. Fritz pointed to the bubbling pool. "Let's get in the pool everyone, the water's fine."

She stepped behind Gillian, and they watched in horror as Ms. Fritz shoved Gillian towards the water. Maren's mother teetered and then stumbled into the pool, her scream gurgling as she went under. The ground shook, and Gillian was gone. Maren started to bawl, and Mateo cried out.

"Perfect!" yelled Ms. Fritz. "Don't worry," she said, waving her hand at Maren. "Mommy's just fine down there, we'll join her soon. Just a test."

Jeremy felt the vibrations well up in his sternum, and he clenched his fists, wanting to blast Ms. Fritz and the IIU into submission so he could rescue his father. But then the incinerator was still pointed at Maren, and the pile of ash that had been a shrub moments ago was still smoldering. Jeremy was paralyzed with indecision.

Wantoro realized his window to do anything helpful was closing. Suddenly, he elbowed the nearest captor in the chin, making him drop his gun. The IIU scrambled for it, but Wantoro bent down and got to it first. He pointed the gun at Ms. Fritz and stood up. He had lived under this woman's thumb for five years, resisting every impulse to fight back so he could see his son again, but maybe that time was over.

"Let's make a trade," Wantoro said to Bentley. "You let us get a head start, and Ms. Fritz gets to keep her head."

Bentley didn't flinch, and continued to train his gun on Maren. "Get in the pool, Wantoro. Fritz is expendable and she knows it. That's part of the deal."

Ms. Fritz grimaced and held her breath.

Wantoro studied Fritz's face, wanting this to be a bluff, but he saw it wasn't and knew he had lost. Jeremy's concern for Maren was equally apparent—he couldn't risk escalating things. Wantoro dropped the gun and looked at Jeremy. "Goodbye, son." He stepped into the pool, and was swallowed by the steam. Two IIU members shoved Mateo in after him, and Maren cried out.

The vibrations in Jeremy's chest roared. Blue lightning burst from Jeremy's hands towards Bentley just as Bentley's finger began to squeeze the incinerator's trigger, and the man dropped the weapon as he was blasted backwards into the pile of ash. Ms. Fritz and the IIU froze for a moment, gaping at Jeremy.

Then from behind them, boots were pounding the cobblestone path. A police officer rounded the corner. "He's over here!" A few more appeared, pistols drawn, flashlights illuminating the strange scene around the pool. "Everyone, put your hands in the air! Do not attempt to run. We will fire if necessary!"

Ms. Fritz held up her hands. "Jeremy, Maren! Things weren't supposed to happen like this. Trust me, Mantel will straighten it all out. If you want to see your parents again, you must jump into the pool! Here is not death, but life! Come, everyone, into the pool!"

The officers, confused, closed in. "Step away from the pool with your hands up!"

Jeremy looked at Maren and beckoned for her. "We have to go in. Maren, she's right. We'll be fine! Let's go to our family."

Maren gave a small nod, and Jeremy took her hands, interlocked his fingers with hers. "Maren, deep breath, okay?"

"But, there's the police and, I-I don't understand what's happening," her voice trailed off as she stepped closer to the hot spring with Jeremy.

Ms. Fritz turned towards the police. "My good officers, please lower your weapons. This is all just a big misunderstanding."

The police ignored Ms. Fritz. "Everyone on the ground, now. Stop walking or we will fire. You in the white, halt!"

The IIU were slowly closing in on Jeremy and Maren, with their hands up. One police officer fired a shot, and a bullet tore through Drew's thigh. Blood splattered his white uniform and he staggered forward.

Jeremy gripped Maren's hands tightly. "Now!" Jeremy jumped into the gurgling green liquid and pulled Maren after him. Lyrna crashed out of a bush, leapt in after them, and disappeared. More shots rang out, and the IIU dropped to the ground.

"He's in!" yelled Jasmine. "Let's go." Ms. Fritz and the IIU members rolled into the pool.

The police exchanged bewildered looks and crept towards the hot spring. The bubbling green liquid seethed. The bottom of the pool, if there was one, was not visible.

An officer held up a radio to his mouth. "We're going to need some backup."

CHAPTER 37

MANTEL'S MAZE

The instant their bodies touched the bubbling green waters, they were enveloped in steam. This passed in a few seconds, and Jeremy, Maren, and Lyrna were free falling in a tunnel. And they were dry. Even more miraculous, they weren't falling so much as they were rapidly floating downward, as if there were an invisible counter-force to gravity cushioning their descent. Jeremy blinked and looked around him. The tunnel had been bored through different layers of rock and soil, and patches of it would light up and go dark at intervals. Every now and then, a chill came over his body.

"Maren, stop screaming. Maren!"

"Huh?" Maren stopped screaming and opened her eyes. "What's going on?" She looked at Jeremy and then at the tunnel wall floating past.

Jeremy touched Maren's shoulder. "We're going to be okay."

"Okay?!"

"I've seen some weird things these past couple of years. Trust me, this is fine. We're going to get through this." Jeremy looked down. Blackness. He swallowed. "Wait, it's forking! This side!" The tunnel suddenly forked into two separate tunnels and Jeremy, Maren, and Lyrna floated down to the left, barely escaping separation.

"Hello," said a wheezing voice from above. It laughed and was joined by the squeal of another.

"Who said that?" Maren pulled Jeremy closer to her. Lyrna slipped in between the two of them and shivered.

"So cold!" said Lyrna.

"Look who's falling from grace." A specter emerged from the gloom and circled the party, leaving a wispy trail. The figure had long fingers, a sunken face, and a huge grin. "Do you see this?" The voice had an echoing quality, like it was coming from a place far away.

"Poor fledglings!" said another, portly ghost, as it popped out of the stone. Jeremy, Maren, and Lyrna screamed in unison.

"They usually come in through volcanos, don't they? We should take them to the catacombs!"

"We mustn't meddle!" said the portly ghost. "The others went to the Heart, maybe *he* wants them?"

"I must say, graveness does not become you!"

At that, the two ghosts burst into laughter and whizzed around. The thinner ghost flew straight through Maren. She gasped.

"What, what are these things," whispered Maren, clutching Jeremy and Lyrna.

"Oh, we're lost souls. Unsorted, as they say. But all the better, we'd have gone to Hell. Ta ta." And the ghosts disappeared back into the walls of the tunnel. Jeremy, Maren and Lyrna kept descending, but their velocity slowed as they approached a stone floor, and then they touched down softly in the chamber of a cave.

"Jeremy!" said Maren. "Ghosts! Where do you think..."

"I don't know." Jeremy looked around. Torches lined the walls of stone corridors that continued on from the chamber. Hundreds of coffins were stacked vertically, fitted into the walls, and covered in cobwebs. The air was damp and cold. "We didn't smash to bits on the ground, so let's just relax."

"Relax! Do you know what's going on? Is this part of your twitchy air, angel thing? Why did we jump into a boiling pool?!" Maren gasped and spun around, half-expecting to see a corpse rise from the nearest coffin. She managed to kick up a thick layer of dust and went into a coughing fit.

"We have to save our parents. Stop fidgeting please. I never told you this, but before we left Watico, Ms. Fritz told me in private that an otherworldly visitor spoke to her, and that I was supposed to go somewhere. This is where I'm supposed to be."

"So what, Ms. Fritz is your ally now?"

"Of course not." Jeremy stepped forward and brushed aside some cobwebs on the nearest coffin. It felt ice cold.

"Don't touch it!"

Jeremy leaned forward and read aloud the inscription:

> *Here lies the remains of Dennis O'Leary.*
> *After haunting Fairview Gardens, the scene of his*
> *murder, Dennis gave his soul to*
> *Mantel in a fine duck*
> *sauce with roasted chestnuts.*

Jeremy shuddered and turned to see Maren's reaction. She had resigned herself to a cautious silence. He read the inscription on the next coffin:

> *Here lies the remains of Anne Sanders.*
> *After searching the entire Eastern seaboard for her*
> *son*
> *Joseph's plane, Anne gave her soul to Mantel stuffed*
> *with*
> *cabbage.*

"Let's get out of here," whispered Maren.

"Door," said Lyrna.

There was a break in the arrangement of coffins and a wooden door was set in the wall a few steps away. Jeremy made his way to the door and motioned for the others to follow. Right before he touched the rusted handle, his foot landed on a slightly raised tile and a loud click came from above. Lyrna hissed. Maren was the first to look up.

"Jeremy, watch out!"

Jeremy looked up and saw white and gray debris falling fast towards him. He jumped back as dust and ash piled up in front of him.

"Jeremy, are you okay?" cried Maren between coughs.

"Yeah! What...?" Jeremy waved his hand in front of his face and squinted through the dust. On the floor in front of him lay a pile of human remains. "Oh, God!" Jeremy gagged.

"What? What is it!"

"Skeletons, Maren. We have to get out of here."

"Skeletons!" she shrieked.

"Door here!" Lyrna clawed at the large wooden door, eager to depart. Maren rushed around the pile of bones and pushed the door open. Light flooded into the catacombs. Jeremy followed and shut the door behind him.

The room was a fifteen-foot square with a torch in each corner and six more wooden doors, each one plain and identical to the other. Jeremy, Maren, and Lyrna picked their way across the stone floor, being careful not to step on any more suspicious tiles.

"Which door?" asked Maren.

Jeremy shrugged and opened the closest door. Behind it was a wall of stone. He tried the next door. Behind it was a steep, dark staircase. Something up the stairs moaned. Jeremy shut the door.

"Maren, why don't you try the next one," he said.

Maren stiffened and walked to the next door. "There were... ghosts." She stood in front of the door for a long time, grabbing its handle, releasing it, and grabbing it again.

"Just do it," goaded Jeremy.

Maren flung the door open and jumped back. There was a dark corridor with a single door at the end. Green smoke seeped through the crack between the floor and the door.

"Let's just get this over with," said Jeremy. He picked up Lyrna and walked down the corridor.

Maren raced down the corridor after him. "Wait! How can you be so sure?"

"I'm not 'so sure,' I'm decisive. Do you want your parents back?"

Lyrna batted at Jeremy's ear. "Scared!"

Their hesitation only made Jeremy want to move faster.

He inched closer to the door, grabbed the handle, pulled, and–

"You're out of the catacombs," said an echoing voice, and the thin ghost from before rose slowly from a pool of bubbling green liquid at the center of the room. "I was hoping you'd join us," it said.

Lyrna wriggled free from Jeremy's arms and ran back to Maren, who clung to the wall just beside the door.

Jeremy made his way to a stalagmite beside the pool that had been fashioned into a seat. Glowing moss grew in patches everywhere in the rocky chamber, casting an eerie light. Jeremy looked down into the green waters and saw the wispy silhouette of the other ghost haunting the depths.

"Okay, we're here now. Is there something you wanted to tell us?" Jeremy shuddered as the thin ghost rose in the air towards him. A flash of red lit up the black of the ghost's eyes.

"When I said I was hoping you'd join us, I meant I was hoping you'd die."

Jeremy opened his mouth to speak but was interrupted by the portly ghost, whose head popped up out of the water.

"Don't look so alarmed," said the specter, winking. "We were rooting for you."

"We thought if your spirits made it out of the catacombs, at least your trace would have weakened."

Jeremy's heart beat fast in his chest. "I've no idea what you're talking about."

The thin ghost passed through Jeremy and he felt a terrible chill. "When you die down here, you attract demons," it said. "The trace of a life departed is strongest at the scene of death. Demons like fresh souls. We don't want to be around when that happens."

"What is this place?" asked Jeremy. He looked behind him at Maren and Lyrna. Both were still as stone, watching from the shadows of the hallway.

"This place," said the thin ghost, "is Mantel's Maze."

Jeremy blinked. "Mantel. I'm supposed to locate him for some reason. Do you know what he wants from me?"

The thin ghost dove from the air and hovered in front of Jeremy's face, giving him a dark grin. "Hmm, can't say for sure. He's always cooking up some plan or another."

The portly ghost stifled a laugh. "You seem like well-seasoned adventurers with... juicy stories."

"I've read the epitaphs!" snapped Jeremy. "Are you saying he wants to eat me?" Jeremy leapt up from the stone seat. The thin ghost flew in front of him.

"Wait," began the thin ghost. "He wants to see you specifically? You're sure about that?"

Jeremy nodded. "But why would he want to eat me?"

The ghost shrugged. "He wants to eat us all. Anyway, it's considered an honor. I'd rather be a ghost, of course, but some souls yearn to be consumed." The specter smacked its chops.

Jeremy looked at Maren and Lyrna to see how they were settling in with this news. Neither spoke, but Maren was glaring at Jeremy as if to remind him that it was his half-baked idea to jump in the pool to begin with.

"Okay," said Jeremy slowly, "and why would the souls yearn to be consumed?"

"Be careful!" warned the portly ghost. "We really shouldn't meddle! Mantel was going to take them to the Heart! We shouldn't have brought them here. You heard it, Mantel wants this meat bag for something, these aren't your average mountaineers!"

"M-mountaineers?" Maren stammered from the hallway, pushing her stringy blonde hair behind her ears. A droplet of moisture fell from the dank ceiling and landed on her nose, causing her to jump.

The thin ghost smiled. "Explorer types. The living tend to enter through volcanoes. The dead are summoned."

"Let's take them to the Heart!" said the thin ghost.

"Please," said Maren, "tell us why souls want to be eaten by Mantel?"

The thin ghost hovered away from the pool and over

to Maren, who retreated slightly into the hallway. "Mantel is great," he whispered with an air of secrecy. "You become a part of Mantel and make him greater. He feeds on souls and that's how he gets his power. It's a sacrifice for the greater good."

"You really shouldn't have said that," said the portly ghost, shaking his head.

"I'm done! This way," said the thin ghost, and beckoned them towards the exit on the other end of the chamber.

Jeremy, Maren, and Lyrna followed the ghosts through the next door and down another long, dark corridor. Maren pulled on Jeremy's sleeve.

"Let's *not* go to Mantel to get eaten?" she whispered.

"We're not going to be eaten. I'm not just some mountaineer. Mantel probably thinks I can tell him something about the Haze. We need to get our parents, then we're out of here, promise."

Lyrna sniffed at a large crack that ran along the base of the wall, and paused to inspect a gaping hole in the stone.

"Hurry up, Lyrna," said Jeremy, motioning for her to join him.

"Eyes," whispered Lyrna, her ears flattened.

Jeremy and Maren shuddered, not wanting to know more.

At last, they arrived at a rusty metal door with Hebrew script scratched onto its surface. Maren recognized the language from her studies, but couldn't read the message. Jeremy opened the door. The room was also made of rusty metal and was dimly lit. An odor of rotting flesh assaulted their nostrils. A corpse was slumped up against the side of the wall. Maren gasped and jumped back. Jeremy turned away and gagged.

"See? A mountaineer," sneered the thin ghost.

"Who did this to her? Did Mantel do this?" asked Jeremy with one hand holding his nose.

"Could have been the giants, or any one of the warlocks. Maybe Ekoto. Likely some Amalgaterra."

"Or Mala'pez." Both ghosts shuddered upon hearing the name.

"Mala'pez?" Jeremy said louder than he meant to, his voice echoing off the metal walls. It worried him that ghosts could fear something. What could be worse than getting eaten by Mantel?

"Keep your voice down.," whispered the thin ghost. "It's a demon. Not the one that haunts the catacombs. This one's faster. I've seen it myself around this level of the Maze." The thin ghost noted the bewilderment on Maren's face and added, "Demons sometimes come in disguised as ghosts. They escape Hell and come here. But when a demon eats a ghost, the ghost goes straight to Hell."

The portly spirit leaned forward. "When you die down here, we recommend the catacombs. Demons love fresh souls, and as my friend pointed out earlier, your ghost has the best chance of, er, surviving if you perish in the catacombs."

Jeremy cast his eyes to the ground.

"Because of the slow demon."

"I get it." Jeremy took Maren by the hand.

The thin ghost nodded and opened another door a crack. They heard the sound of chains tightening and slackening.

The thin ghost turned around and whispered to the portly ghost, "I think Belvdor is sleeping."

Maren shivered. "Who... what's that?"

"Belvdor," said the thin ghost, "is one of Mantel's Amalgaterras. Mantel experiments with building new beings out of soul remains."

Just then, a deep-voiced incantation rumbled into the rusty metal chamber from behind them. It was coming from the room with the green pool. The ghosts' sunken eyes flashed red and their jaws dropped, revealing a blackness within. "It's Mala'pez!" cried the thin ghost. "Sorry! You're on your own!" The two ghosts vanished into a wall.

CHAPTER 38

Diabolus Mos Eat Vos Lost Animus

"Mala'pez! The, the fast demon?" Maren quaked from head to toe. She peaked her head into the next room with the sleeping Amalgaterra, and then retreated. "So two choices," Maren whispered, hating that this conversation was happening in an echoey metal chamber. She took a deep breath. "We can go forward and try to get past this sleeping monster, or we can retreat and risk running into, er, the fast demon."

"I say we take the sleeping monster. It's chained down so we stand a chance."

"What if we pass it but the door is locked?" Maren scooted her back against the wall until she brushed up against Jeremy.

"I check." Lyrna licked Jeremy's hand. "Small, quick."

Mala'pez groaned from somewhere behind them.

"Okay, Lyrna. But be careful." They all crept forward and peaked past the metal door. Slumped over on the floor in the next room was a creature the size of an elephant, its skin a dappled arrangement of fur and scales. It looked like a cross between a wolverine and a Komodo dragon. Its chest was rising and falling rhythmically, and a raw, animal odor now mixed with the putrescence of the corpse.

Lyrna slinked across the floor as the creature's large, leathery tail whipped towards her. Lyrna dodged backwards as the tail slapped the stone, and the fizdruft narrowly missed hopping onto the creature's back paw. The door was five feet away.

Lyrna looked back at Jeremy and Maren in the doorway.

Jeremy nodded in encouragement.

Lyrna crept towards the door. But the Amalgaterra's tail flicked again and landed on Lyrna's back. Her feline instincts got the best of her and she hissed and spat indignantly, immediately regretting it. Belvdor snuffled and opened its red eyes, which rolled in their sockets and settled on the small, furry intruder. Chains rattled as it lumbered to its feet and a guttural sound came from its chest like an old engine starting. It bared its butcher-knife teeth and slime oozed from its mouth. Its slitted pupils rolled to the back of its head.

Lyrna leapt into the air and gave Belvdor's reptilian nose a nice scratch before she skittered back to the room with the corpse. Belvdor howled, its voice like metal scraping metal. The monster surged against its chains, which strained and snapped, and it crashed into the metal doorway, denting it with its impact. But Belvdor was too large to get through, and could only swipe inside the metal room with its paw. Being unable to reach the intruders, Belvdor grew frustrated and began pacing around its chamber.

"Quick, close the door!" shouted Maren.

"Just go!" Jeremy pushed Maren into Belvdor's chamber. The monster snorted and charged at them, but Jeremy pulled Maren to the side, brushing past Belvdor, who slammed into the doorway again. "Run!" barked Jeremy.

As they bounded towards the exit that may or may not be locked, Jeremy could feel Belvdor's hot, rancid breath on his neck. He spun around and saw the butcher-knife teeth gnashing towards him. His hand crackled and he rained lightning into the creature's open mouth. Belvdor stumbled back and shook its head like a dog, stunned for a moment. Then it roared and raged forward.

Maren was at the exit now, trying the rusty door handle, but it was stuck. She jostled it desperately. Belvdor was charging again, his dark shape blotting out the light in the room, looming closer, threatening to crush them with pure momentum. In the nick of time, Maren pushed down the door handle, the door opened, and they scrambled through it, slamming it shut. There was a massive thud, and for a moment they were afraid the door would buckle, but it held.

They raced down the corridor and through the first door on the left. To their horror, the demon Mala'pez's otherworldly incantations were now growing louder, and they went back out that door. Jeremy flung the next door open. "Down here!"

The door opened to a long, descending staircase, and Jeremy, Maren, and Lyrna clambered down. When they got to the base of the stairs, they quieted. Maren's hands fumbled for Jeremy. The room was so dark, her eyes had trouble adjusting. "Do you hear it?" she whispered.

"I think so." Jeremy looked up. A faint light trickled in from behind the door at the top of the staircase. The demon's incantations were coming from above. The sound was alien, and had so much bass it made the stones beneath their feet vibrate.

"DIABOLUS ERO ALIVE ITERUM. DIABOLUS MOS EAT VOS LOST ANIMUS. REDEO UT VERSUS INCENDIA."

"Jeremy! It's Latin." Maren crouched on the ground and hugged her knees. "Our souls, it wants our souls!"

Jeremy flinched. The door at the top of the stairs creaked open, and the incantation amplified to a painful volume.

"It's coming down the stairs! We have to move!" Maren sprang up and rushed forward into the blackness. She banged against something and fell.

"Maren?" Jeremy felt around in front of him.

"DIABOLUS ERO ALIVE ITERUM. DIABOLUS MOS EAT VOS LOST ANIMUS. REDEO UT VERSUS INCENDIA."

"I think I'm bleeding," cried Maren.

"Light!" mewed Lyrna. Jeremy felt her claws sink into his leg.

"I know, I can't see!"

"No, lightning!"

"Ah!" Jeremy crept in the darkness towards where Maren had fallen. He held one hand out in front of him to prevent a collision and brought the other up over his head. They heard heavy rattling on the stairs.

Concentrate. A blue spark danced in his hand. He shot it up to the ceiling. The temporary blue flash revealed that Maren had tripped over a rusty stone brick oven. She rose to her feet. "Do it again!"

"DIABOLUS ERO ALIVE ITERUM. DIABOLUS MOS EAT VOS LOST ANIMUS. REDEO UT VERSUS INCENDIA." Now it was at the bottom of the steps.

"Again!" said Lyrna.

Jeremy produced a ball of electricity and held it in his palm, his face tense with concentration. Lyrna ran forward.

"Here! Room."

Maren and Jeremy followed Lyrna. The next room was lit by torches and Jeremy allowed the ball in his palm to fizzle.

"Your power is incredible." Maren gaped at Jeremy.

He yanked her forward and ran.

After opening and closing some fifteen odd doors, Jeremy collapsed onto the floor, heaving and sweaty. They no longer heard the incantation. Maren and Lyrna curled up beside him and there they stayed for some time, quiet and afraid some new creature would stumble upon them. The room was small and plain, with stone tiles and walls and three wooden doors. A lamp was placed beside the smallest door just in front of them.

"I think we're safe here," said Jeremy.

"Lightning. You make lightning." Maren stared in wonder at Jeremy's hand.

"I do."

"I guess all that air twitching paid off?" She smiled weakly but then sniffled.

"How's your cut?" asked Jeremy, feeling protective.

"It's not too bad." She lifted up her pajama bottoms to reveal a small gash just below her knee. "I need to clean it. At least it stopped bleeding."

Jeremy stood up and stretched. There was a stitch in his side. "Yeow, I'm thirsty."

"We're going to die," said Maren morosely.

"We're not going to die, Maren." There was an edge to his voice. "We just have to get to the Heart."

"This is a maze, it's not like if we keep opening and closing doors we'll get there!"

"I toffee," said Lyrna sadly. She sniffed the floor in vain.

"I'd like some toffee too." Maren stood up and attempted to brush the dust and grime off her chick pajamas. "So we're here because Mantel wants to eat you?"

"We don't know that."

"Well then what *do* you know?"

"We have the same information, Maren. Ms. Fritz sent me to find Mantel years ago. We're in a maze underground. He builds mazes and eats souls. Demons float around, monsters are everywhere. We'll figure it out." Jeremy walked over to the door with the lamp beside it and opened it. The room looked much the same as the others, with four identical wooden doors, and stone floors and walls. "Pick one."

Maren rubbed her eyes and sighed. "That one." She pointed to one of the doors and Jeremy opened it. An old man in rags was standing up against the door and toppled over.

CHAPTER 39

CIRCLE OF WISDOM

"Pardon me!" yelled the old man from the floor.

Jeremy helped him to his feet and eyed him curiously. The old man wore what seemed to be a potato sack with holes in it, and his white, stringy hair sprouted everywhere.

"That's right, I'm no demon. Name's Fedonis." The old man shuffled over to a makeshift stand set up in the corner of the room. Jars of potions and talismans lined the shelves. He grabbed a comb from his wooden counter and yanked it through his stringy hair. "Damn humidity," he mumbled. "So what will it be today, hrm?" He grinned a toothless smile.

Lyrna ran up to the stand. "Water? Food?" She hopped from paw to paw.

"Don't know where the oasis is located, hrm? It's a map you'll be needing!"

Jeremy and Maren exchanged looks and joined Lyrna by the stand.

Fedonis rustled through a drawer and pulled out an aged map. It was made of tan hide and large chunks were missing, as though it had been chewed. "Get you all around! Get you to your oasis, this will. What do you have for me?"

Jeremy frowned. "I'm not sure I understand you. Do you... accept credit cards?"

"Credit what?" The old man leaned across the counter and gave Jeremy a great sniff. "Let's see it."

Repulsed, Jeremy took a step back and pulled his credit card from his wallet. He pushed it across the counter, missing the old man's extended hand on purpose. Maren kicked Jeremy's foot disapprovingly.

The old man grabbed the credit card and examined it with a magnifying glass. "What does it do, exactly?"

"You can buy anything you want with it. It's linked to a bank. I have a $25,000 credit limit."

"$25,000!" gawked Maren.

"Manhattan Bank, where's that?" asked the old man, who was examining the thickness of the card.

"Manhattan, New York... Earth–"

"It's an Earth thing?"

"Er, yes."

"I'll take it!" Fedonis shoved the card into his pocket and held the map out to Jeremy.

Jeremy winced at losing so precious a commodity, but accepted the map.

"Now that map's only local, shows a couple levels, of course. But what else will it be? Have lupin spine? I got the cure for you right here!" He dangled a red-orange potion in Maren's face.

Maren held up her hand to push the potion away from her face. "I was wondering if you could answer a couple of questions for us."

"What, so it's information you're wanting? Ah!" The old man bustled out from behind his makeshift storefront and ambled over to another corner of the room. He sat on a wooden stool and placed a blue, pointy wizard's hat on his head. "Welcome, welcome, to Fedonis the Hermit's Circle of Wisdom.

"But–"

"Ah, ah, ah, young man. You must answer my riddle correctly and then you may ask me anything you'd like." The old man whistled his own theme song, holding up a finger and retreating it only after the song reached its conclusion.

Jeremy's heart was softened by this amiable display of insanity and he laughed aloud. "Let's hear the riddle."

The old man cracked his knuckles and gave each of his guests a serious stare in turn. "Visit my family tree and you'll see cousins of brown and black. I am white and naked, with lots of fur along my back. What am I? Teehee."

Maren recited the riddle again. She motioned for Jeremy and Lyrna to join her in the center of the room.

"Fur like animal," said Lyrna hopefully.

"Yes, I think it's an animal. Something to do with a family tree."

"Monkeys?" offered Lyrna.

"Black monkeys, chimps. Um..." Maren looked to Jeremy.

"Aren't there monkeys with naked butts?" He smiled.

"Yes, very mature," said Maren. "One species is snow monkeys."

"That makes sense."

Maren considered this. "It does, but to say the snow monkey is naked except for the fur on its back seems imprecise."

"Yeah, but maybe its whole underside is naked. It's a riddle, Maren, it's not rocket science. There's word play, puns..."

"Puns! A polar bear?"

"Huh?"

"There're brown bears and black bears," said Maren. "It's white and naked, which is another way of saying it's bare, or *a* bear, and it's furry!"

"But what about the family tree thing?"

Maren walked up to Fedonis and stood in front of his stool. "The answer is polar bear."

"Are you sure?" asked the old man, touching the top of his hat and glaring his best glare.

"Yes, polar bear."

"Correct." He whistled his theme song.

Jeremy and Lyrna joined Maren in front of the hermit and waited patiently for the song's conclusion.

When at last the song concluded, Fedonis wagged his finger. "Ah, ah then. Let's have the question."

"Who or what is Mantel?" said Jeremy, stepping forward.

"Who or what is Mantel," repeated the hermit, drawing out the letters as though he were tasting each one. "Mantel was once a soul, like so many others you find in this maze. But when he went to be sorted after his death, God couldn't decide where to place him, so he kept him in the Haze where he floated all alone. Ah, but who was he? He was called Cain. Cain!" The hermit chewed on the side of his mouth.

"Cain?" said Jeremy, astonished. "As in–"

"Cain murdered his brother Abel and died some time later himself. Yes, he was *that* Cain. Ah, so then he stayed in the Haze, angry and confused, until a haughty angel took pity on him and said, 'Cain, I see your fate is not fair. Did you not honor the Lord and receive punishment in return?' So, the angel returned Cain's soul to his body. His body decomposed but his consciousness lived on, tethered to his bones.

"Ah, but then one night, Cain noticed there was a spirit haunting the graveyard and he called it over to him.

240

When the ghost was close enough–" Fedonis chomped the air with his toothless mouth and stared at Maren, who quivered. "Mantel ate the ghost and gained its power. Of course, it's not eating like you and I know it. He must completely subdue the will of the soul, until it yields to his own and the energy is digested and incorporated into his being. He continued calling souls to him–ah yes, see the dead who haunt the earth are lonely and easily summoned.

"After he gained immense power, he traveled to the center of the earth where he could have a proper kingdom. He called himself Mantel, and allowed other souls to live with him. He proclaimed that if the ghosts joined forces with him, that they could avoid being sorted in the Haze. Why, he asked, would they want a union with God only to lose their individuality? Why risk going to Hell to suffer eternal damnation? Many ghosts joined Mantel and together they built Mantel's Maze. Ah, and his forces are growing, but they're still no match for God or Lucifer. There simply aren't enough souls who haunt the Earth after death." The old man pointed to his hat to signify that he was finishing up and began to squirm his way off the stool.

"Wait!" cried Jeremy. He trained his electric blue eyes on Fedonis.

"Yes, my good boy?"

"So is Mantel good or bad? I mean, you seem like a nice person."

"Teehee! Good or bad? Person! Phooey! Neither and neither!" Fedonis jumped down from his stool and walked back to his storefront. "What will it be today, then?"

"He's obviously bad, Jeremy! He eats souls!" Maren threw her hands up.

Lyrna tugged on Jeremy's pants. "Leave now!"

Jeremy clenched his fist. "What does he want with me?"

"Let's have a look at that map," said Maren, her hands outstretched.

It showed an oasis that was only a couple of doors away.

Jeremy tapped his chin. "We'll stop at the oasis and then continue through here. Then we'll take the passageway upstairs to avoid this place." Jeremy pointed to a large, black spot on the map marked 'Kellaware's Dungeon.' "The more direct route would be to stay on this level until we're under the Heart, but I'd rather bypass the dungeon. I don't even want to know what kind of monsters lurk around there. If we take the passageway, we'll arrive at the Heart of the maze from the southern entrance."

CHAPTER 40

BEASTIE

Jeremy, Maren, and Lyrna arrived at the oasis. They walked through a thicket of ferns and moss to a pool bubbling in the center, which sprayed a fine mist onto their skin. The pool had a rainbow hue and light shone up from the bottom. Across the waters was a small, fawn-like creature drinking from the pool. It looked up with dewy eyes and then darted towards a door. It stood upright to turn the handle, and then lowered gracefully back onto its hoofs before scurrying out.

"That was kind of cute," said Maren, sitting next to the pool. She cupped her hands, dipped them into the waters, and took a sip. The liquid tasted like a citrus punch and she drank greedily. When she finished, she sat against a rock and watched Jeremy and Lyrna refresh themselves.

Jeremy's sweat-soaked shirt and disheveled hair made him look more masculine than she thought possible. He'd always been fit, but seemed delicate. Still, his entitled and moody demeanor eroded his charm. She especially didn't appreciate the way he handled her, pushing her and pulling her like a rag doll.

Maren was also frustrated by Jeremy's lack of skepticism as to why Mantel wanted him. He had to know something after everything he'd gone through. Was she willing to die for him? Of course not. But she felt like if she continued to have a relationship with him, whatever it was, beyond this terrifying ordeal, she would likely die at his side. Jeremy was intriguing but ultimately a destructive force. No, that part of him hadn't changed, she concluded. And she felt guilty for this.

"Maren," said Jeremy, interrupting her musings. "I just realized how tired I am. It looks like we have a ways to go on the map, so we should camp out."

"I–"

"I was thinking we can camp either here by the oasis or the next door over. I know it's dangerous, but this area of the maze seems reasonably safe. That old man set up a storefront and that's saying something."

Maren frowned. She was only going to say that she was tired too.

Jeremy led everyone to a cavernous room. A faint light trickled down from somewhere above, and the walls seemed to climb up indefinitely. The floor was jigsawed with large stone tiles. They chose a corner of deep shadow to set up camp. Jeremy made a pillow with a pile of ferns from the other room, and was fast asleep.

Maren was on watch. She felt herself nodding off but would rouse herself, feeling a little shot of adrenaline each time she imagined some evil entity creeping into the chamber. But eventually she couldn't fight sleep. She rubbed her eyes and laid on a dusty slab of stone that was slightly elevated, hoping that a creepy-crawly insect or snake might decide it not worth its while to ascend the tile to get to its inhabitant. When at last she convinced herself that she was safe enough, she dozed off.

"Maren! Maren, wake up!" Jeremy shook her.

Maren's eyes opened wide. "What! I'm sorry! I didn't mean to fall asleep!" she cried, jumping up from her stone tile.

"Don't be sorry. Look at what you're sleeping on. I've been trying to figure it out for the past ten minutes, but I couldn't wait any longer." Jeremy pushed Maren's leg off the edge of the tile.

"It just looks like a stone tile," said Maren, holding her head. "How long did I sleep?"

"I don't know, long enough." Jeremy called Lyrna to his side. "Think you can stick your paws in here and help loosen it? There's something underneath."

Lyrna shook her head. "Too scared!"

"Scared? Lyrna, it's a rock. It's inanimate."

"Under stone!"

"There might be tuna fish under the stone."

"Tuna, happy!" Lyrna danced on her paws.

Maren sighed. "There's no tuna fish under there, Lyrna. Come here." She patted her lap and Lyrna joined her.

Jeremy bent over. "Look! There's a picture etched into the stone. See here? On the top? You didn't notice this last night, Maren?" He brushed the dust off with his hand.

"No, I didn't," said Maren irritably.

"Beastie!" said Lyrna.

"What is it?" asked Maren, mildly interested.

"Maren, check this out!"

Maren crouched down for a better look at the tile. "Don't touch it!" She grabbed his hand. Jeremy laughed.

"Will you relax? It's a—"

"Beastie!" mewed Lyrna from the corner.

"Yes, you could say that.... It looks like that monster from Looney Tunes! What was it called? The big, orange hairy one. Maren, did you ever watch Looney Tunes on Earth?"

"Beastie..."

"Gossamer!" continued Jeremy. "It means goose summer. Supposed to be ironic."

Maren shook her head.

"I had a lot of free time at Ms. Donegall's, okay?"

"Maybe you shouldn't mess with it. Let's get out of here." Maren rubbed her arms and looked up. There was a massive wooden door hung slightly ajar about twenty feet into the air on the wall. "Jeremy, do you see that? Why would there be a door up there?"

"Crazy," said Jeremy. He began chipping away at the base of the tile. "Look! I was right, something's down here." He gripped below the tile.

"Tuna?!" chirped Lyrna. She leapt into the air and spun around, a few drops of drool splattering on the floor.

"No, no there's something inside the stone under this tile. It's a box! Help me dig some other tiles up so we can get this box. I could probably tip the top sideways, and..."

The offer didn't appeal to Lyrna and, disappointed, she settled next to Maren, who was beginning to feel anxious.

Jeremy continued uprooting the tiles. He lifted up the now loosened slab and pushed it aside, revealing a box in a stone compartment in the floor. It was a cardboard box just big enough for Jeremy to sit in. Inside was a set of huge drawing chalks, each the length of Jeremy's arm. He broke a few into smaller pieces and set them on the floor. Jeremy smiled and then lifted the box up for Maren and Lyrna to see.

"Jeremy, let's go."

"Maren, can I have a moment?"

"With the box?" Maren blinked.

"Yes, with the box. Is that okay?" Jeremy took up a piece of chalk and drew a goose on the side of the box and scrawled out a message. He then read it aloud: "For Gossomer, in Honor of the Monster Tile."

"Bizarre, Jeremy." Maren smiled. She remembered being seven years old and playing with Jeremy inside his parents' art room. She had some good times with him growing up, in between all the weird ones.

Jeremy sat in his box. "Now, a song." He cleared his throat and winked at Maren:

> Far away in a maze,
> There sits a monster tile.
> We arrived from the Haze
> And it took us quite a while,
> To hear the ghost tell a ruse
> And buy a map from a quack,
> But because I've drawn a goose,
> We'll ward off an attack.

Just then, a door at the other end of the chamber creaked open. Maren gasped and Lyrna hissed. Jeremy went silent.

A bright light spilled into the room, then adjusted to

a softer glow. A hand appeared in the doorway holding a lamp.

"Hello?" said a low, strong voice. A man stood in the doorway. "Hello? Hi guys!"

"Hello...?" said Maren, rubbing her eyes.

"Hello! Sorry for bursting in like that, neighbor!" A young man with black, close-cropped hair stood before them, the white letters of his lacrosse sweatshirt matching his brilliant teeth. He let out a hearty laugh. "My name's Steven. There are six of us at a camp site a couple doors down. I thought I heard some–" Steven looked directly at Jeremy, who was still sitting in his box, "singing. Some voice, eh?" Steven smiled at Maren. She gave a guarded smile back. Jeremy only raised an eyebrow and feigned an interest in his nails.

"I'm Maren. This is Lyrna and that's Jeremy."

Steven walked into the room and knelt down in front of Lyrna. "Lyrna, is it? What a great-looking critter."

"Thanks," said Lyrna. Steven jumped back.

"She can talk! I tell you, this maze is full of surprises. Anyways, great to meet you." Steven offered his hand to Maren, who shook it awkwardly. Then Steven held his hand out to Jeremy for a while, but Jeremy kept his arms crossed and eventually gave Steven a small nod. "Okay. Well hey, we have a ton of food at our site and you guys are welcome to it."

Jeremy rose from his box, clapping the chalk from off his pants. "Maren and Lyrna are both ladies. They probably don't like that expression–you know, using the term "guys" interchangeably for both men and women. I know I can't stand it."

Maren ignored Jeremy. "Thank you, Steven. I haven't eaten in so long."

"We stopped at the oasis," said Jeremy, stepping out of his goose box.

"The oasis is all fine and well, but wait 'til you see what

we have at our camp!" Steven laughed and punched the air with his fist.

"I'll be glad to be around more people," said Maren. She suspiciously eyed his immaculate presentation. "Did you, er, fall into a volcano?"

"Sure did. I was hiking with some friends on Mt. Saint Helen a year or so ago when we fell into the mouth. We were standing there taking pictures when the ground collapsed beneath us. You?"

"Oh, well we fell into a hot spring," said Maren. She looked to Jeremy for support.

"We jumped into the hot spring, actually."

Steven smiled. "We'll all swap stories. Love finding newcomers. You'll see what I mean about the food. Won't believe it 'til you taste it. My lady." Steven opened the door for Maren. Lyrna followed. Jeremy frowned and picked up his box and chalks.

"Jeremy, are you really bringing that box?" asked Maren.

"We have cots to sleep on, fella." Steven's smile wilted a little when his eyes met the goose drawing.

Jeremy proudly hoisted his box over his shoulder and walked through the door, pausing briefly to allow the goose drawing to linger in Steven's face.

CHAPTER 41

THE DUNGEON

Jeremy, Maren, and Lyrna followed Steven through a series of doors. Steven kept a grueling pace and Maren had to jog to keep up.

"Hey Steven," said Jeremy. "I thought you said you were next door."

"I am. We're in a maze and sometimes next door isn't exactly a stroll down the block, know what I mean?"

Jeremy cursed Steven under his breath. He had never gotten along well with other guys and this one was no exception. Maren heard Jeremy curse and nudged his shoulder.

"What's wrong?" she whispered.

"Who is this idiot?" said Jeremy.

"He seems like a nice guy, but we should probably be careful."

"You especially."

"Me?"

"He's going to grab you like this." Jeremy set his box of chalks down and grabbed Maren, throwing her over his shoulder. She struggled and laughed because he'd tickled her.

"Is everything all right?" said Steven, stopping to inspect the shenanigans.

"Put me down." Maren's cheeks flushed.

"Embarrass," said Lyrna.

"I was just playing. She's out of breath, you're moving too fast." Jeremy placed Maren back on the ground.

"Oh?" said Steven.

"Jeremy, I'm fine. You're both just taking wider strides than me, but I can keep up."

"But your cheeks are red," said Jeremy. He leaned against the wall of the corridor and crossed his arms. "You're out of breath."

"I'm fine, you were just tickling me!" Maren jogged away from Jeremy and caught up to Steven.

A few minutes later, they went through a carved wooden door and into a hall that had been prepared for a feast. Long tables were set with silver cutlery, and a crystal chandelier hung from the ceiling. A gold statue near one wall depicted a harvest scene. The whole room smelled like rose water.

"Finally, someone in this godforsaken dungeon has paid attention to aesthetics," said Jeremy, taking a seat at the end of one of the banquet tables and placing his box on the floor beside him. He took a deep breath. "And what a beautiful smell." Jeremy motioned for Maren to join him at the table. She hesitated and then took a seat beside him.

"So where's the food?" Jeremy brushed Maren's hair behind her ear and smiled.

Maren pulled away.

"Are you not feeling well? You keep turning red."

"You're so friggin' handsy! Stop, Jeremy. Just stop." Maren slid down the bench away from Jeremy. "Steven, where are your friends?"

"They must be out hunting," said Steven dreamily. "Don't worry, when they return we're sure to have a feast."

Jeremy called for Lyrna to join him and she jumped up onto the padded bench. He pulled the map out from his pocket. "So where are we on here?" He ran his finger across the map. "Should I mark it?" Jeremy smiled and pet the top of Lyrna's head. He picked up a large yellow chalk from his box.

"You've got a map?" Steven moved towards Jeremy for a closer look.

"Yes, and you haven't? Of course you know this place by heart and are probably best pals with all sorts of freaky-ass creatures."

"Jeremy!" said Maren.

"We're looking for the Heart of the maze, Steve, so if you could just point it out to us...."

Steven smiled. "It's above us."

"So that would mean we're..." Jeremy moved his finger across the map, "third level, right next to the dungeon." He fixed his eyes on Steven, who stood smiling and unblinking before him. "That seems like a dangerous place for a banquet," he said slowly.

Lyrna flattened her ears and hissed. They heard a muffled clanking coming through a door behind the harvest statue. Jeremy and Maren both jumped to their feet. The door flew open, and a grunting monster burst through, clad in crude armor and brandishing an axe. Jeremy, Maren, and Lyrna bolted for the exit as more creatures streamed into the room. On her way to the door, Maren slipped on a piece of yellow chalk that Jeremy had dropped on the ground, falling hard on her backside.

Jeremy turned just as the first monster reached Maren. Its face was human-like, but horribly misshapen and scarred. Maren tried to scramble to her feet but her attacker took a coiled net off its back and flung it over her. Her limbs became entangled and as she stood, she slipped on the chalk and fell again, this time landing on her face with a sickening thud. The abomination howled.

Jeremy's hands were shaking. He charged the creature, running in a tight arc to attack it from the side. The abomination lifted its ax halfway, but Jeremy was too quick. He leapt and deflected the blade harmlessly with the bottom of his foot while grabbing the creature's head with both of his hands. It stumbled backwards and Jeremy landed on top of it, still gripping the misshapen head. Electricity spiraled down his arms and poured into the skull, disintegrating the twisted brain from within.

Lyrna was busy distracting four other creatures. They lunged and swung their weapons at her, but Lyrna ducked and dodged, and the blades whiffed around in the air. When she saw that one of the monsters was off balance, she counterattacked with her claws, raking the flesh between the gaps in its armor. This enraged it, and the monstrous creature swung harder. It had over-extended and was bent forward, so Lyrna leapt and sunk her claws into its dull eye. The creature howled and spun. But Lyrna's claw was stuck and she was whipped around, catching an axe blade through the last inch of her tail, which lopped off and fell to the floor.

Lyrna was finally thrown free, and she screeched and crawled under the table. Another creature jumped and landed in the middle of the table, cracking the wood and scattering cutlery everywhere.

Jeremy, seeing the bloody stump of Lyrna's tail on the ground, yelled out. His hair stood on end as the vibrations welled up in him, and he swept his arms and hurled a wave of energy into the monsters, who were making their way towards Lyrna. The wave bowled them over, and they were stunned for the moment. Maren had finally climbed out of the net and was standing in the exit, shouting.

Jeremy and Lyrna joined Maren in the doorway, and they ran in a frenzy down the hall.

They raced through the maze, opening and closing doors indiscriminately. After ten minutes of running, Maren closed a door and turned to Jeremy. "We left him," she said between breaths. "Steven!"

"That was a set-up, Maren. He was with them."

"You don't know that. Steven could be dead!"

"I killed one of those creatures, Maren! Did you see?" Jeremy's eyes shone wildly. "I didn't know—I never imagined…"

"I... don't know what I saw." Maren looked at the ground and then up at Jeremy. She wiped her hair from off her face. "But thank you."

A moment of silence passed between them.

Jeremy bent down beside Lyrna and ripped the bottom of his shirt off. He wound it tightly around the tip of her tail. The fur of her tail was slick and matted with blood. "Lyrna, I was so afraid you left me." Jeremy scooped Lyrna up and hugged her close to his chest.

Lyrna mewed affectionately.

Maren rubbed her eyes. "Jeremy, you brought the chalk?"

"Apparently." Jeremy examined his hands and saw that they were covered in a yellow dusting. He felt in his back jean pockets and produced two large pieces of chalk. "But not the map." He slammed his fist onto the stone wall and cursed. Lyrna flattened her ears.

"But okay," said Lyrna. "Still alive." She tugged at his pant leg with her mouth, got a tongueful of chalk, and then heaved and spit.

"It's not okay."

"We shouldn't have left Steven," repeated Maren sadly.

"Maren, it was a set up. We weren't 'next door' to where he found us. We were beside the dungeon, the one place I knew for sure that I wanted to avoid. But you were all smitten with him calling you a guy and holding the door for you and being a general weirdo." Jeremy walked to the opposite stone wall and began to doodle geese pictures with the yellow piece of chalk.

"Okay! So maybe it was a set up. Sorry for being concerned about another human being's welfare." Maren stood up and started pacing the room.

"And I'm not? I've been looking out for you since we've been here! I could leave at any time if I wanted."

"Really? Well I wouldn't be here if it weren't for you!"

"So you don't want to see your parents?"

"You know what I mean, I wouldn't have come to Earth if I hadn't gone with you on Failrun!"

Jeremy held his breath and doodled furiously. First he drew a flock of geese in the sky. Then he drew a pond and added a mother goose and her goslings.

"Jeremy."

He continued to ignore her and started on a sunset.

"Jeremy, put the chalk down."

"Chalk!"

Jeremy turned around and was about to tell Lyrna not to get involved when he saw a large yellow creature with mangy fur descending the wall. Jeremy immediately recognized it as the monster on the tile. Before he could warn Maren and Lyrna, the creature had sprung down to the center of the room, knocking Maren to the floor. It stood on its hind legs like a gorilla and roared, bearing its black teeth and leering at Jeremy.

Jeremy stumbled back and dropped the chalk. It rolled behind him.

"Chalk!" roared the creature, and licked its lips with a forked tongue.

"It wants the chalk, give it the chalk!" Maren crawled to the furthermost wall and watched in horror as Jeremy flung the chalk at the monster. The chalk smacked the monster in the head and it toppled over. When it lifted its large furry head, it clapped its hands. "Good chalk! Make Urm happy!"

Maren blinked. She looked to Jeremy, who stood up warily. "Is it... friendly?"

Lyrna approached the monster from its side, her ears tucked back. "Urm, I Lyrna."

The monster beat its chest. "Urm."

"Is that your chalk, Urm?" asked Jeremy.

The yellow monster shook its head. "Yes, mean ghost hid it. I look for long time. Say I'm stupid."

Maren inched over to Jeremy with her back against the wall. "We don't think you're stupid."

"Thank you, friends!" Urm jumped up and down, lifting his furry legs to his chest and slamming them to the floor. "Urm love chalk!" Urm crawled up the craggy wall, his left arm firmly holding his chalk. He began to draw self-portraits.

"Let's leave. Now." Maren tugged at Jeremy's shirt and they tiptoed to the door.

"Psst, Lyrna!" said Jeremy.

"Wait!" Urm crashed to the ground. "Where you go?"

"Heart!" said Lyrna cheerfully.

"Lyrna, come on!" Jeremy motioned for Lyrna to exit the room.

"Heart? Wait! I take you there. Very simple. Hop on back." Urm patted his back and crouched on the ground. "I take you up wall, through high door to Heart now."

Jeremy examined the walls and saw that there was a door thirty feet up. He pointed this out to Maren.

"It might make things easier." He shrugged.

"Wait!" said Maren. "Do we really want to go to the Heart? Let's think this through. What happens there?"

The monster raised its bushy eyebrow. "Heart Mantel's throne. You want eat, right?"

"No I do not want to be eaten! Jeremy, what are we doing?"

Jeremy put his hands on the monster's yellow back and vaulted up into a riding position. Lyrna clambered up Urm's leg. "Maren." Jeremy patted Urm's fur, indicating a seat in front of him.

Urm gave Maren a black-toothed grin. "Manren, I waiting."

"Jeremy, I don't know." Maren closed her eyes and shook her head.

"Maren." He patted Urm's fur again. "Unless, of course, you wanted to sit on my lap." He smiled.

Maren gasped. "Jeremy!"

"Don't act so shocked."

Maren couldn't believe his trespass, especially under the current circumstances. "This is serious, we could die!"

"Exactly. Get up here."

Maren sighed and reluctantly climbed onto the yellow monster's back. "All right, but this is for my parents' sake."

CHAPTER 42

MANTEL

Urm sprang up onto the stone wall, his massive paws finding holds in its cracks and protrusions. Jeremy and Maren held tight to Urm's shoulders, and Lyrna did the same on Jeremy's back. The monster climbed until he reached a great wooden door with a heart engraved just above the handle. "Ready?" asked Urm.

Jeremy sighed. "Yes."

Urm opened the door and pulled them onto a perch that overlooked a circular chamber. The room's floor was black marble inlaid with precious stones glinting in a spiral pattern. Sitting at the room's far end was a gilded throne and a tapestry depicting a harvest. And huddled against a blood-red wall, disheveled and bound in chains, were Jeremy and Maren's parents.

"Jeremy!" shouted Wantoro.

"Father, what's going on down there?"

"Jeremy, watch out!" Wantoro shook his chains.

Jeremy and Maren gripped Urm's fur as he descended the wall. "Wait, Urm!"

But Urm had already reached the bottom. He shook them off his fur and leapt back onto the wall. "Urm go now!" Urm scurried up the blood-red wall and disappeared behind the wooden door.

"Wait!" Maren yelled.

"Jeremy Chikalto," said a strange voice. The words vibrated in two dissonant octaves, rumbling like thunder and at the same time shrill as a rusted hinge.

From behind the tapestry came a shriveled, fleshy figure robed in black. Its body emanated waves that disturbed the air surrounding it, like the heart of a fire. It hovered above the ground and loomed towards Jeremy.

"Yes, Mantel. This is the boy you seek." Ms. Fritz now emerged from behind the throne. She smoothed her hair to her head and smiled.

"Maren, you have to get out of here!" yelled Gillian from across the room, tears streaming down her face.

Mantel's hood fell back and Maren gasped. His head was pale and wrinkled, with coal-black eyes and a flat nose with flared nostrils. He raised one hand, an iridescent stump with finger buds. "Jeremy Chikalto, descendent of Vordin Chikalto, I am honored."

"What?" Jeremy stammered.

"Some ghosts led you astray. My apologies." Mantel lowered his hand.

Jeremy glanced at his father, who looked fierce despite his shackles. Jeremy balled his hand into a fist. "I'm here now, so what do you want?"

In a flash, Mantel manifested in front of Jeremy, inches from his face. Jeremy fell back on the floor and Mantel hissed with laughter. "Jeremy Chikalto, do not worry about your friends and family. It is you who I want. Look at me." Mantel's dark stare bore down on Jeremy's soul like an anchor. He drew his face closer to Jeremy's, almost touching. Jeremy tried to jerk his head away but found that he could not, and he was transfixed by Mantel's visage.

Beneath the waxen skin was a ghastly collage, tiny faces bubbling up and blistering under the pink flesh. An eye blinked beneath Mantel's cheek; a mouth screamed on his forehead. The faces of the dead were roiling inside him. Then a shrill voice pierced Jeremy's head, cutting all thoughts off at their root, omnipresent.

"Yes, I was once called Cain. But do you know who are?"

Everything around Jeremy warbled. Out of the corner of his eye, he saw Lyrna throwing herself against the air, as though a forcefield separated her from him and Mantel.

Don't hurt us, thought Jeremy. Sweat dripped down his brow and mixed with the tears forming on his eyelashes.

"Hurt you?" said the voice in Jeremy's head. Mantel rose and circled Jeremy, leaving a trail of pink mucous on the black marble. Jeremy struggled to his feet, but found he couldn't walk, and stood rooted to the floor as Mantel revolved around him.

"Vordin Chikalto was my salvation," continued Mantel. "He showed me mercy and took my damned, unsorted soul out of the Haze. Like the angel Gabriel, he heralded new life; like the Anointed One, I rose again and offer life."

How did—

"Vordin Chikalto was like you."

Jeremy's eyes widened. *But...*

"Angel blood runs in your veins."

And my father?

"Only you."

Jeremy struggled against the voice again, forcing his eyes down onto the black polished floor.

"Jeremy Chikalto!"

You're hurting me! His temples were tensing up, twisting into knots, and his mind felt a terrible pressure building, as though his head might explode.

"Don't resist. Be with me. You must cross over to the Haze and gather souls for my harvest."

Jeremy dropped to his hands and knees and gnashed his teeth, the pain was so excruciating. *Why should I bring you souls?!*

"You can live here, with me. I will fulfill you. What do you desire? Wealth, power... love?"

Souls are supposed to be sorted in the Haze.

"The Apocalypse is imminent. We must be ready." Mantel's lips curled. "Ah, I see. Your thoughts betray you. You think you are allied with God?" Mantel laughed and a black smoke billowed from his mouth. "I'm afraid you are predestined to choose between my company or Lucifer's. God does not want you." Mantel drifted behind Jeremy and whispered in his ear. "It isn't fair, I know. God's vengeance is durable. After your ancestor took pity on me and returned me to my corpse, he was cursed. You embody that curse."

That doesn't make sense. Jeremy gritted his teeth.

"Few comprehend the divine agenda." Mantel's shrill voice had entered Jeremy's head again. "I too bear the mark of a curse. See?" Mantel pointed to his neck with his iridescent finger buds. Over a web of blue and purple veins, Jeremy saw a tattoo. Two black spirals were joined at the center, bisected by a blue line that looped at the end.

Mantel's mouth twitched. "God cursed Vordin Chikalto for his trespass on the divine will. You are the fruition of that curse. You, with the smug fantasy of God's grace, are to aid the fallen Lucifer in unleashing the greatest darkness. You, Apollyon."

I don't believe you. Jeremy closed his eyes and held his head.

"You are the Angel of the Bottomless Pit. But you have a choice, there is always a choice. Join me and we can rise up against Lucifer's army at the end of days. We can topple God!" Mantel's eyes shimmered and light bent and twisted around him.

Stop it! Jeremy palmed his temples and forced his head to the ground. He fell forward, his chin cracking on the stone, and blood pooled from his ears. Everything went black. When he came to his senses, he heard Maren screaming.

The IIU had arrived in their starch white uniforms, and were surrounding Wantoro, Gillian, and Mateo.

"Mantel, should we take them to the dungeon?" Bentley looked up from his thick brow and smiled.

"That's up to Jeremy. Tell me, Apollyon, are they enemies or guests?" Mantel gestured to Wantoro with his frail, pink hand. "Unchain him."

Bentley nodded and unchained Wantoro.

"Jeremy, you were saying? Enemies or guests?"

"They're nothing to you."

Mantel let out a splintering laugh and floated to the center of the room.

Jeremy got to his feet and the IIU drew their weapons.

"Jeremy, watch out!" yelled Maren.

Jeremy turned to her, and she was breathless and shaking.

"Jeremy, I will be a perfect host to your loved ones. Stay," crooned Mantel.

"We're leaving," said Jeremy, clenching his teeth. He walked resolutely to Maren and took her hand, then marched to his friends and family. Ms. Fritz laughed.

"But you came here to rescue your father, yes? I imagine someone will die if you ignore my associates."

Bentley clicked the safety off his gun. The other IIU members followed his example.

"No, we're leaving this *place*."

"To the Haze? Really? They wouldn't survive the transition. You know that."

Jeremy looked away. Mantel was right.

"Ms. Fritz, you and the IIU are excused. Your work is done," said Mantel shortly.

Ms. Fritz, Bentley, Jasmine, and Drew exchanged looks, bowed, and then cautiously retreated from the throne room. The door clicked behind them and an uneasy silence filled the air.

Lyrna growled. "No hurt anyone!"

Mantel raised a sickly finger bud. "Oh? Let me escalate this negotiation." He pointed at Lyrna, who was now frozen in the air, caught leaping towards Mantel with her teeth bared, a tableau of the fizdruft, hunter of evil things. Out of Mantel's finger erupted a jet of fire, which blazed so hot Jeremy could feel his skin burning even from a distance. He cried out and ran to the inferno, but it was too late.

When the flames receded he felt a wave of disbelief, but the wave pushed out into its zenith, and then rolled back, sucking him into dark waters, a dread undertow. His beloved pet, his companion and guardian since childhood, the only one who had accepted him entirely, flaws and all, a being of love and loyalty, was now reduced to a pile of ashes. Black and white cinders swirled towards Jeremy, who fell to his knees and raked at the ashes, weeping into the dust. "Lyrna!" Jeremy moaned and the air in the room warbled and pulsed, the waves swelling larger with each cycle.

"Why would you destroy what is so innocent? Oh Lyrna, I'm so sorry!" said Jeremy, his voice cracked and thick. Jeremy turned his back to his terrified friends and family, his chest heaving, rage seething like a volcano, nerves on fire. "YOU MONSTER!" he bellowed, and his blue eyes lit up like beacons. Jeremy's body buzzed and crackled, his hair standing on end. A globe of blue energy exploded around him and then retracted, like the life cycle of a star. Then a supercharged beam burst from Jeremy's sternum and struck

Mantel in the chest. Mantel was blasted back into the blood-red wall, smashing a crater into it, and then fell to the floor, his fetus-like legs rolling beneath him.

"There's a surprise," said Mantel, rising back into the air. He opened his mouth wide and belched. Oozing out of Mantel's stretched orifice was a blackened soul, covered in bile, and all the light in the room vanished. In the darkness a stench of vomit and corruption pervaded the room. The soul slithered towards Wantoro and Jeremy's eyes flashed again. Lightning burst from the center of Jeremy's forehead and struck the looming shadow, stunning it for a moment. But then the soul pressed forward.

Mantel laughed with a thousand voices, growling and shrieking and screaming and whispering, echoing through his vast maze. "Do not resist our alliance! Do not be foolish!"

Mantel rose high and hovered towards his captives, his body vacuuming up the light and air. His coal-black eyes bore into Jeremy, and he belched out another charred soul.

Jeremy could feel pressure on his temples squeezing like a vise, a pain so sharp it almost blotted out everything else, but he fought it, tried to push it aside, tried to be outside himself. This was it. His father was going to die, Maren and her parents were going to die. Lyrna was gone, and never again would he hold her warm body in his arms, press her soft fur to his face, feel her gentle weight on his legs as he slept.

He knew what he must do. If his father, Maren, and her parents were going to die, he'd rather it be by his hands. He'd rather they die in the Haze, where they could be sorted into some afterlife and not doomed to wander this Godforsaken maze or be eaten by Mantel. As Mantel's shadow deepened over him, he rushed to his loved ones, hugged them, enveloped them in his thoughts. He felt his father's sturdy frame, and Maren's slender one next to her wiry mother, and Mateo's big arms were around him, and they huddled together in the storm rampaging around them.

Jeremy could feel Mantel's grip on his temples loosen and the Cajjez slowed his breathing. *Concentrate.* Deep inside of him, a pool of still water began to whirl, flowing faster and faster around its gyre, its funnel growing into a tornado, the storm inside eclipsing the one outside. Then the vibrations exploded through Jeremy, and a rope attached to his sternum whipped him into the beyond. He opened his eyes in the Haze. His father, Maren, and her parents floated beside him, unconscious in the inky purple atmosphere.

Jeremy took his father's hand and pulled him close. Shallow breaths rose and fell from the great chest, and Jeremy felt the pulse deaden in his fingertips. The Haze stretched on indefinitely before them, and Jeremy picked a direction and swam forward. If he could just find somewhere to pull them out, they might live.

"Help!" Jeremy saw an elk trotting past and swam to it. From a cord clenched in its teeth, the elk hauled the body of a little girl whose face was blue from frost. She cried as the elk led her to her ultimate destination. "Help! I have living souls with me! I need to get them out!" The elk shook its head and trotted on.

They were now in the thick of the Haze, clouds obscuring everything in front of them. Jeremy spun himself around and forgot which way was up and which way was down. He didn't even know the direction he'd come from. He swam with his father's limp body tucked under his right arm and Maren under his left, exhausted, a lone lifeguard who had been swept out to sea. He had been forced to leave Gillian and Mateo behind.

Any minute now, a spiritual creature would approach them to take his father and Maren to their afterlife. Would he be responsible for their deaths? Would this count as murder?

Then something was approaching from the gloom, an outline of a creature. It drifted forward quietly and Jeremy closed his eyes. He did not want to witness death's departure. *Here it comes. Goodbye father. Goodbye Maren.* He held his breath. A cold sensation brushed his cheek.

"Jeremy!"

Jeremy opened his eyes. Lyrna mewed.

"Lyrna!" Jeremy grabbed Lyrna and held her close to him, stroking her fur. Instead of the warm body he was accustomed to, she was cool like the Haze, but he felt her essence intact, a clean spirit. "I'm so sorry! Lyrna, I wanted to pet you one last time!"

"Ferry souls, me!"

"Oh, Lyrna! Have you come to take my father and Maren from me?" Jeremy held his father's limp body up. "Please be quick."

"No, Wantoro alive." Lyrna pushed her head up under his large hand. "Trouble breathing."

"He'll die soon then," said Jeremy sadly.

"Yes." Lyrna paused. "But Lyrna know! Mom!"

"He'll join my mom."

"No, mom *here*!"

"I know, I saw her when she died."

"No, mom here and there, Watico. You see. Call her!" Lyrna pranced around.

Jeremy frowned and looked at Maren. "Is Maren dead?"

"No! Call mom! Coma. Not dead, not alive. Connect to Watico. Follow voice and leave Haze!"

Jeremy felt a song play on his ear, the faint chime of a piano. "What's that?"

"Yes, concentrate!" mewed Lyrna, bouncing from paw to paw.

It was his mother's song, the tender harmony before the sweep. Then a clear voice joined the chimes, like a stream trickling over rocks. Jeremy turned in the direction of the music. "Mom?" He looked at Lyrna, astonished. "Is that?"

"I get Mateo and Gillian! You call, go, I follow! She dream in-between."

Jeremy pulled his father and Maren forward, swimming through the purple clouds with renewed vigor. "Mom!" he called out. "Mom, please?"

His mother stopped singing. "Jeremy? Is that you? I sense you, are you here?"

"Mom! Where are you!" Jeremy drifted towards her voice.

"I don't know! Jeremy?"

"Mom!" Jeremy flew into a fold in space and the Haze opened up sideways. Over a shimmering crack between the Haze and a place beyond, a brown bear stood vigil, holding a glowing blue cord in its teeth. The rest of the cord ran into the crack and disappeared. The bear was waiting patiently for something.

"Mom?"

The cord tugged and fell limp again. Jeremy followed it into the crack, still holding Maren and Wantoro in either arm. The bear watched them impassively. "Lyrna, I think I found her!" he called back, before pushing the three of them into the crack. He felt a buzz as they passed through a membrane of energy and popped out the other side, tumbling onto solid floor. "Mom!"

Raaychila lay stretched out on a hospital bed. Machines and tubes connected her to life, and there was a steady beeping. "Mom! It's me! Can you hear me?" Jeremy laid Wantoro and Maren on the floor and opened the hospital door. "Can somebody help! My father's not breathing!"

A doctor rushed into the room just as Jeremy disappeared back into the Haze.

Back in the purple swirls, Lyrna raced towards Jeremy, towing Mateo and Gillian by their cords. Jeremy reached out and grabbed Mateo by his big arms. Then he reached for Gillian.

"No," said Lyrna. She tucked her ears back and gently tugged Gillian's cord away. He looked at her still face, her sharp features now placid, and knew Gillian was gone.

Lyrna motioned towards the rip in space. "Mateo need air, quick."

Jeremy hesitated. "Thank you, Lyrna." He pulled Mateo through.

CHAPTER 43

ALIVE

Jeremy sat at his father's bedside in the Watico Medical Center's Emergency Room. Instead of the charcoal stone and ragged torchlight of Mantel's Maze, everything was now cream-colored and pastel green. Wantoro slowly opened his eyes.

"Good morning, Father." Jeremy smiled and squeezed Wantoro's hand.

"Jeremy! Where am I? Are you okay?"

"We're back on Watico. I'm fine. The nurses brought this." Jeremy stood up and wheeled a cart to Wantoro's side. He lifted the lid of a platter to reveal a lobster, mashed potatoes, and a citrus salad. "You should see the mobs outside. The press is unbelievable."

"You've grown so much." Wantoro squinted up at Jeremy. "I went to find you. The IIU–"

"Father, please." Jeremy stood up and shook his head. He reached deep into his pockets and pulled out a small chunk of yellow chalk. There was a knock on the door.

"Come in," said Jeremy.

"Cajjez Jeremy, you have another call from Maren Nononia in room 503."

Jeremy hesitated. "Uh, no, I won't be taking it. Please, just—I'll get back to her later." He took a deep breath and cast his eyes to the floor. He couldn't face her yet.

"Understood, sir." The nurse closed the door.

Jeremy straightened. "But dad, now that you're awake, I wanted to show you that we have a visitor." He set his yellow chalk on the bedside desk and then pulled back a curtain.

A nurse wheeled Raaychila into the room.

"Is she…?"

"She's still in a coma, but she's alive."

Wantoro looked from his son, now a handsome young man, to his lovely wife. "I've traced the lines of her face in my mind's eye so many times these last five years."

Jeremy felt the warmth of love surround him. He smiled and rapped his fingers on the desk before picking up his yellow chalk and writing on a loose piece of paper, "I'm sorry." But then the air twitched and a feeling was leaking out of the Haze, washing over him, a vast emptiness like the silence of an arrested horn, full of fury, waiting to blare its doomsday song.

Be sure to check out these other books in The Hazy Souls series!

Jeremy Chikalto and the Hazy Souls
(Book 1 of The Hazy Souls)

Jeremy Chikalto and Leviathan Island
(Book 2 of The Hazy Souls)

Jeremy Chikalto and the Demon Trace
(Book 3 of The Hazy Souls)

With more tie-ins coming soon!

Follow us online:
www.viralcathouse.com
tsdebrosse.blogspot.com
www.facebook.com/tsdebrosse/
Twitter @YAFiction